18. 10. 83

EVERYMAN, I will go with thee,

and be thy guide,

In thy most need to go by thy side

DYLAN THOMAS

Born in Swansea, 22 October 1914. Died in New York, 9 November 1953. Buried at Laugharne, Wales.

QUITE EARLY ONE MORNING

broadcasts by

DYLAN THOMAS

preface by

ANEIRIN TALFAN DAVIES

Welsh Region, B.B.C.

DENT: LONDON, MELBOURNE AND TORONTO
EVERYMAN'S LIBRARY
DUTTON: NEW YORK

Printed in Great Britain
by Biddles Ltd,
Guildford, Surrey
for
J. M. Dent & Sons Ltd
Aldine House, Albemarle Street, London
First published in 1954
Aldine Paperback edition 1967
Reprinted 1968, 1971, 1974
Everyman Paperback 1978

No. 1007 Paperback ISBN 0 460 01007 7

CONTENTS

This collection of radio material falls naturally into two categories, represented by the two parts of this volume. In the first we have his creative work, talks and the 'talks-feature' 'Return Journey,' and in the second radio talks of a more didactic nature, together with extracts culled from radio discussions, and introductions to poetry readings. In making extracts from discussions I have attempted to select those which stand more or less independently of the context of the discussion itself.

A. T. D.

page

Preface vii

PART I

Reminiscences of Childhood (*First Version*) 1

Reminiscences of Childhood (*Second Version*) 8

Quite Early One Morning 15

Memories of Christmas 21

Holiday Memory 29

How to begin a Story 38

The Crumbs of One Man's Year 43

The Festival Exhibition, 1951 50

The International Eisteddfod 58

A Visit to America 63

Laugharne 70

Return Journey 73

PART II

	page
Wilfred Owen	91
Walter de la Mare as a Prose Writer	106
Sir Philip Sidney	112
A Dearth of Comic Writers	122
The English Festival of Spoken Poetry	126
On Reading One's Own Poems	130
Welsh Poets	139
Wales and the Artist	153
Three Poems	155
On Poetry	168
Notes	171

PREFACE

This collection of radio scripts by Dylan Thomas constitutes with *Under Milk Wood*,[1] already published, all that can be preserved in print of his contribution to the broadcasting medium in this country. Fortunately, the rest of that contribution, his skill as broadcaster and poetry reader, has in some part been saved for us by recordings.

Through the microphone, as writer or reader, Thomas made his art and personality widely known, and drew into the circle of his readers many whose appreciation of his verse needed the persuasion of the poet's own interpretation; in this way the number of readers and admirers grew, until, as the sales of the *Collected Poems*[1] show, the popularity of Thomas's work was unequalled by any other modern poetry in English.

But for Thomas the broadcasting medium played a still more important part in leading his work towards greater clarity and directness. As he himself said:

> It is impossible to be too clear. I am trying for more clarity now. At first I thought it enough to leave an impression of sound and feeling and let the meaning seep in later, but since I have been giving these broadcasts and reading other men's poetry as well as my own, I find it better to have more meaning at first reading.

To hear Dylan Thomas read poetry or deliver one of

[1] See the list of works printed at the beginning of this volume.

his talks was an unforgettable experience. His voice, remarkable in variety and range, was at its most impressive when the opportunity arose to display its still more remarkable resonance. His poem, 'Ceremony After a Fire Raid,'[1] for example, gave such an opportunity, and his reading of the closing liturgical lines was most majestic. The occasion of this recording was, to me, most memorable. Thomas sat before the microphone in the Swansea studio, a forgotten cigarette stub in his fingers, his shoulders thrust back, his chest bulging out from his oversized jacket and displaying a vast expanse of rumpled shirt, while, in contrast to this almost comic picture, there came from his mouth like thunder made articulate

> The masses of the sea under
> The masses of the infant bearing sea
> Erupt, fountain, and enter to utter for ever
> Glory glory glory
> The sundering ultimate kingdom of Genesis' thunder.

Thomas was well aware of the dangers of this noble style of delivery, and, in moments of self-criticism, referred to himself as a 'second-rate Charles Laughton' or a mere 'man with the gift of the gab.' No one should be deceived by this. However thin the dividing line between the good and the bad, Thomas was on the right side of it; in him eloquence was not grandiloquent, and grandeur escaped pomposity. His readings showed the sensitiveness and sure discrimination natural to the poet, and, with these, a knowledge that could be acquired only by close study; what Thomas gave his hearers was not merely an impressive performance or a successful

[1] See *Collected Poems*, p. 129.

interpretation, but a revelation of the poet's creative impulse.

In the evaluation of Thomas's art as a script writer there is the same danger of underestimating the amount of consideration and industry that went into the work. The catalogues of nouns and adjectives, conceits and puns, which at first seem haphazard, casual, or improvised, reveal to closer examination the deliberate skill of the craftsman who weighed every word and every syllable. For this reason, perhaps, the number of his scripts is out of all proportion to his fame as a script writer. John Arlott, who produced many of Thomas's poetry readings, has called attention to the comparative rarity of his broadcasts, and to another strange fact, that most of these were not broadcast centrally.

> He made his considerable reputation in sound broadcasting on the basis of much less than the crowded regularity of appearance of most well-known broadcasters. From his first programme in 1937 until after the war, his radio appearances were almost all for the Welsh region of the B.B.C.

If the radio scripts printed in this volume are read in chronological order, a development in the technique of the writer can be distinctly traced. There is space here to mention only one aspect of that development, the approach to a very original form of radio drama. The course of this movement can be marked from *Quite Early One Morning*, through *Return Journey*, to *Under Milk Wood*, where, by leaving the stage himself, the poet has taken the step from dialogue to drama. This is the end, or the arbitrary interruption of death, according to opinion. Thomas himself had less than complete confidence in his ability as a dramatist. When, in 1938, he was invited by a producer in the Welsh Region of the B.B.C. to write a dramatic feature in verse, he replied:

> I don't think I'd be able to do one of those long dramatic programmes in verse; I take such a long time in writing anything, and the result, dramatically, is too often like a man shouting under the sea.

But this lack of confidence, as we have seen, proved wrong in the event. Even had the discipline of stage drama proved too austere, radio drama would still have offered Thomas the best opportunity for his gifts of characterization and humour, and his mastery of the visual and evocative power of words.

ANEIRIN TALFAN DAVIES.

1954.

ACKNOWLEDGMENTS

For permission to print the following poems read by Dylan Thomas in the course of his broadcasts grateful acknowledgments are made to Messrs Jonathan Cape Ltd (*The Inquest* and *The Bust* by W. H. Davies), Mrs Idris Davies ('O what can you give me?' by Idris Davies), Messrs George Allen & Unwin Ltd ('Sacco Writes to his Son' from *Ha! Ha! among the Trumpets* by Alun Lewis), the executors of Wilfred Owen and Messrs Chatto & Windus Ltd (*Exposure*, *Anthem for Doomed Youth*, *Greater Love*, *A Terre*, and *Strange Meeting* by Wilfred Owen), the Fortune Press and Mr Glyn Jones (*Esyllt* by Glyn Jones).

Dylan Thomas's own poems, as read, are also reprinted here by arrangement with his literary executors.

PART I

Reminiscences of Childhood

(*First Version*)

I was born in a large Welsh industrial town at the beginning of the Great War: an ugly, lovely town (or so it was, and is, to me), crawling, sprawling, slummed, unplanned, jerry-villa'd, and smug-suburbed by the side of a long and splendid-curving shore where truant boys and sandfield boys and old anonymous men, in the tatters and hangovers of a hundred charity suits, beachcombed, idled, and paddled, watched the dock-bound boats, threw stones into the sea for the barking, outcast dogs, and, on Saturday summer afternoons, listened to the militant music of salvation and hell-fire preached from a soap-box.

This sea town was my world; outside, a *strange* Wales, coal-pitted, mountained, river run, full, so far as I knew, of choirs and sheep and story-book tall hats, moved about its business which was none of mine; beyond that unknown Wales lay England, which was London, and a country called 'The Front' from which many of our neighbours never came back. At the beginning, the only 'front' I knew was the little lobby before our front door; I could not understand how so many people never returned from there; but later I grew to know more, though still without understanding, and carried a wooden rifle in Cwmdonkin Park and shot down the invisible, unknown enemy like a flock of wild birds. And the park itself was a world within the world of the sea town; quite near where I lived, so near that on summer evenings I could listen, in my bed, to the voices of other children playing ball on the sloping, paper-littered bank; the park was full of terrors and treasures. The face of one old man who sat, summer and winter, on the same bench looking over the swanned reservoir, I can see more clearly than the city-street faces I saw an *hour* ago: and years later I wrote a poem about, and for, this never, by me, to-be-forgotten 'Hunchback in the Park.'[1]

The hunchback in the park,
A solitary mister
Propped between trees and water
From the opening of the garden lock
That lets the trees and water enter
Until the Sunday-sombre bell at dark,

Eating bread from a newspaper,
Drinking water from the chained cup
That the children filled with gravel
In the fountain basin where I sailed my ship,
Slept at night in a dog-kennel
But nobody chained him up.

Like the park birds he came early,
Like the water he sat down,
And Mister, they called, Hey Mister,
The truant boys from the town
Running when he had heard them clearly
On out of sound,

Past lake and rockery,
Laughing when he shook his paper,
Through the loud zoo of the willow groves,

[1] *Collected Poems*, p. 111.

Hunchbacked in mockery
Dodging the park-keeper
With his stick that picked up leaves.

And the old dog sleeper,
Alone between nurses and swans
While the boys among willows
Made the tigers jump out of their eyes
To roar on the rockery stones
And the groves were blue with sailors.

Made all day until bell-time
A woman's figure without fault
Straight as a young elm,
Straight and tall from his crooked bones
That she might stand in the night
After the locks and the chains

All night in the unmade park
After the railings and shrubberies,
The birds, the grass, the trees and the lake,
And the wild boys innocent as strawberries,
Had followed the hunchback
To his kennel in the dark.

And that park grew up with me; that small, interior world widened as I learned its names and its boundaries; as I discovered new refuges and ambushes in its miniature woods and jungles, hidden homes and lairs for the multitudes of the young, for cowboys and Indians and, most sinister of all, for the far-off race of the Mormons, a people who every night rode on nightmares through my bedroom. In that small, iron-railed universe of rockery, gravel-path, playbank, bowling-green, bandstand, reservoir, chrysanthemum garden, where an ancient keeper known as Smoky was the tyrannous and whiskered snake in the grass one must keep off, I endured, with pleasure, the first agonies of unrequited love, the first slow boiling in the belly of a bad poem, the strutting and raven-locked self-dramatization of what, at the time, seemed incurable adolescence. I wrote then, in a poem never to be published:

> See, on gravel paths under the harpstrung trees,
> Feeling the summer wind, hearing the swans,
> Leaning from windows over a length of lawns,
> On tumbling hills admiring the sea,
> I am alone, alone complain to the stars.
> Who are his friends? The wind is his friend,
> The glow-worm lights his darkness, and
> The snail tells of coming rain.

But several years even before those lines, I had written:

> Where could I ever listen for the sound of seas asleep,
> Or the cold and graceful song of a swan that dies and
> wakes,
> Where could I ever hear the cypress speak in its
> sleep,
> And cling to a manhood of flowers, and sing the
> unapproachable lakes?

I am afraid the answer was, the park. (I had 'the swan' on the brain in those days; luckily, there were very few rhymes for 'parrot.') The answer was, the park; a bit of bush and flowerbed and lawn in a snug, smug, trim, middling-prosperous suburb of my utterly confining outer world, that splendidly ugly sea town where, with my friends, I used to dawdle on half-holidays along the bent and Devon-facing seashore, hoping for corpses or gold watches or the skull of a sheep or a message in a bottle to be washed up in the wrack; or where we used to wander, whistling and being rude to strangers, through the packed streets, stale as station sandwiches, around the impressive gas-works and the slaughter-house, past the blackened monuments of civic pride and the museum, which should have been in a museum; where we scratched at a kind of cricket on the bald and cindery surface of the recreation-ground, or winked at unapproachably old girls of fifteen or sixteen on the promenade opposite; where we took a tram that shook like an iron jelly down from our neat homes to the gaunt pier, there to clamber *under* the pier, hanging perilously on its skeleton-legs; or to run along to the end where patient men with the seaward eyes of the dockside unemployed, capped and mufflered, dangling from their mouths pipes that had long gone out, angled over the edge for unpleasant tasting fish. Never *was* there such a town as ours, I thought, as we fought on the sand-hills with the boys that our mothers called 'common,' or dared each other up the scaffolding of half-built houses, soon to be called Laburnums or the Beeches, near the residential districts where the solider business families 'dined' at half past seven and never drew the curtains. Never *was* there such a town (I thought) for the smell of fish and chips on Saturday nights; for the Saturday afternoon cinema matinées where we shouted and hissed our threepences away; for the crowds in the streets, with leeks in their pockets, on international nights, for the singing that gushed from the smoky doorways of the pubs in the quarters we never should have visited; for the park, the inexhaustibly ridiculous and mysterious, the bushy Red-Indian-hiding park, where the hunchback sat alone, images of perfection in his head, and 'the groves were blue with sailors.'

The recollections of childhood have no order; of all those every-coloured and shifting scented shoals that move below the surface of the moment of recollection, one, two, indiscriminately, suddenly, dart up out of their revolving waters into the present air: immortal flying-fish.

So I remember that never was there such a dame-school as ours: so firm and kind and smelling of galoshes, with the sweet and fumbled music of the piano-lessons drifting down from upstairs to the lonely schoolroom where only the sometimes tearful wicked sat over undone sums or to repent a little crime, the pulling of a girl's hair during geography, the sly shin-kick under the table during prayers. Behind the school was a narrow lane where the oldest and boldest threw pebbles at windows, scuffled and boasted, lied about their relations—

'My father's got a chauffeur.'

'What's he want a chauffeur for, he hasn't got a car.'

'My father's the richest man in Swansea.'

'My father's the richest man in Wales.'

'My father's the richest man in the world'—

and smoked the butt-ends of cigarettes, turned green, went home, and had little appetite for tea.

The lane was the place to tell your secrets; if you did not have any, you invented them; I had few. Occasionally, now, I dream that I am turning, after school, into the lane of confidences where I say to the children of my class: 'At last I have a secret.'

'What is it? What is it?'

'I can fly!' And when they do not believe me, I flap

my arms like a large, stout bird and slowly leave the ground, only a few inches at first, then gaining air until I fly, like Dracula in a schoolboy cap, level with the windows of the school, peering in until the mistress at the piano screams, and the metronome falls with a clout to the ground, stops, and there is no more Time; and I fly over the trees and chimneys of my town, over the dockyards, skimming the masts and funnels; over Inkerman Street and Sebastopol Street and the street of the man-capped women hurrying to the Jug and Bottle with a fish-frail full of empties; over the trees of the eternal park, where a brass band shakes the leaves and sends them showering down on to the nurses and the children, the cripples and the out-of-work. This is only a dream. The ugly, lovely, at least to me, town is alive, exciting and real though war has made a hideous hole in it. I do not need to remember a dream. The reality is there. The fine, live people, the spirit of Wales itself.

Reminiscences of Childhood

(*Second Version*)

I like very much people telling me about their childhood, but they'll have to be quick or else I'll be telling them about mine.

I was born in a large Welsh town at the beginning of the Great War—an ugly, lovely town, or so it was and is to me; crawling, sprawling by a long and splendid curving shore where truant boys and Sandfield boys and old men from nowhere, beachcombed, idled, and paddled, watched the dock-bound ships or the ships steaming away into wonder and India, magic and China, countries bright with oranges and loud with lions, threw stones into the sea for the barking outcast dogs; made castles and forts and harbours and race tracks in the sand; and on Saturday summer afternoons listened to the brass band, watched the Punch and Judy, or hung about on the fringes of the crowd to hear the fierce religious speakers who shouted at the sea, as though it were wicked and wrong to roll in and out like that, white-horsed and full of fishes.

One man, I remember, used to take off his hat and set fire to his hair every now and then, but I do not remember what it proved, if it proved anything at all, except that he was a very interesting man.

This sea-town was my world; outside a strange Wales, coal-pitted, mountained, river run, full so far as I knew, of choirs and football teams and sheep and story-book tall black hats and red flannel petticoats, moved about its business which was none of mine.

Beyond that unknown Wales with its wild names like peals of bells in the darkness, and its mountain men clothed in the skins of animals perhaps and always singing, lay England which was London and the country called the Front, from which many of our neighbours never came back. It was a country to which only young men travelled.

At the beginning the only front I knew was the little lobby before our front door. I could not understand how so many people never returned from there, but later I grew to know more, though still without understanding, and carried a wooden rifle in the park and shot down the invisible unknown enemy like a flock of wild birds. And the park itself was a world within the world of the sea town. Quite near where I lived, so near that on summer evenings I could listen in my bed to the voices of older children playing ball on the sloping paper-littered bank, the park was full of terrors and treasures. Though it was only a little park, it held within its borders of old tall trees, notched with our names and shabby from our climbing, as many secret places, caverns and forests, prairies and deserts, as a country somewhere at the end of the sea.

And though we would explore it one day, armed and desperate, from end to end, from the robbers' den to the pirates' cabin, the highwayman's inn to the cattle ranch, or the hidden room in the undergrowth, where we held beetle races, and lit the wood fires and roasted potatoes and talked about Africa and the makes of motor-cars, yet still the next day it remained as unexplored as the Poles —a country just born and always changing.

There were many secret societies but you could belong only to one, and in blood or red ink, and a rusty pocket-knife, with, of course, an instrument to remove stones from horses' feet, you signed your name at the foot of a terrible document, swore death to all the other societies, crossed your heart that you would divulge no secret and that if you did, you would consent to torture by slow fire, and undertook to carry out by yourself a feat of either daring or endurance. You could take your choice: would you climb to the top of the tallest and most dangerous tree, and from there hurl stones and insults at grown-up passers-by, especially postmen, or any other men in uniform? Or would you ring every doorbell in the terrace, not forgetting the doorbell of the man with the red face who kept dogs and ran fast? Or would you swim in the reservoir, which was forbidden and had angry swans, or would you eat a whole old jam jar full of mud?

There were many more alternatives. I chose one of endurance and for half an hour, it may have been longer or shorter, held up off the ground a very heavy broken pram we had found in a bush. I thought my back would break and the half-hour felt like a day, but I preferred it to braving the red face and the dogs, or to swallowing tadpoles.

We knew every inhabitant of the park; every regular visitor; every nursemaid; every gardener; every old man. We knew the hour when the alarming retired policeman came in to look at the dahlias and the hour when the old lady arrived in the bath-chair with six pekinese, and a pale girl to read aloud to her. I think she read the newspaper, but we always said she read the *Wizard*. The face of the old man who sat summer and winter on the bench looking over the reservoir, I can see clearly now and I wrote a poem long long after I'd left the park and the seatown called: 'The Hunchback in the Park.'

The Hunchback in the Park
A solitary mister
Propped between trees and water
From the opening of the garden lock
That lets the trees and water enter
Until the Sunday sombre bell at dark.

Eating bread from a newspaper
Drinking water from the chained cup
That the children filled with gravel
In the fountain basin where I sailed my ship
Slept at night in a dog kennel
But nobody chained him up.

Like the park birds he came early
Like the water he sat down
And Mister they called Hey mister
The truant boys from the town
Running when he had heard them clearly
On out of sound

Past lake and rockery
Laughing when he shook his paper
Through the loud zoo of the willow groves
Hunchbacked in mockery
Dodging the park keeper
With his stick that picked up leaves.

And the old dog sleeper
Alone between nurses and swans
While the boys among willows
Made the tigers jump out of their eyes
To roar on the rockery stones
And the groves were blue with sailors.

Made all day until bell time
A woman's figure without fault
Straight as a young elm
Straight and tall from his crooked bones
That she might stand in the night
After the locks and the chains

All night in the unmade park
After the railings and shrubberies
The birds the grass the trees and the lake
And the wild boys innocent as strawberries
Had followed the hunchback
To his kennel in the dark.

And that park grew up with me; that small world widened as I learned its secrets and boundaries, as I discovered new refuges and ambushes in its woods and jungles; hidden homes and lairs for the multitudes of imagination, for cowboys and Indians, and the tall terrible half-people who rode on nightmares through my bedroom. But it was not the only world—that world of rockery, gravel path, playbank, bowling-green, bandstands, reservoir, dahlia garden, where an ancient keeper, known as Smoky, was the whiskered snake in the grass one must keep off. There was another world where with my friends I used to dawdle on half holidays along the bent and Devon-facing seashore, hoping for gold watches or the skull of a sheep or a message in a bottle to be washed up with the tide; and another where we used to wander whistling through the packed streets, stale as station sandwiches, round the impressive gas-works and the slaughter-house, past by the blackened monuments and the museum that should have been in a museum. Or we scratched at a kind of cricket on the bald and cindery surface of the recreation ground, or we took a tram that shook like an iron jelly down to the gaunt pier, there to clamber under the pier, hanging perilously on to its skeleton legs or to run along to the end where patient men with the seaward eyes of the dockside unemployed capped and mufflered, dangling from their mouths pipes that had long gone out, angled over the edge for unpleasant tasting fish.

Never was there such a town as ours, I thought, as we fought on the sand-hills with rough boys or dared each other to climb up the scaffolding of half-built houses soon to be called Laburnum or The Beeches. Never was there such a town, I thought, for the smell of fish and chips on Saturday evenings; for the Saturday afternoon cinema matinées where we shouted and hissed our threepences away; for the crowds in the streets with leeks in their hats on international nights; for the park, the inexhaustible and mysterious, bushy Red-Indian hiding park where the hunchback sat alone and the groves were blue with sailors. The memories of childhood have no order, and so I remember that never was there such a dame school as ours, so firm and kind and smelling of galoshes, with the sweet and fumbled music of the piano lessons drifting down from upstairs to the lonely schoolroom, where only the sometimes tearful wicked sat over undone sums, or to repent a little crime—the pulling of a girl's hair during geography, the sly shin-kick under the table during English literature. Behind the school was a narrow lane where only the oldest and boldest threw pebbles at windows, scuffled and boasted, fibbed about their relations:

'My father's got a chauffeur.'

'What's he want a chauffeur for, he hasn't got a car.'

'My father's the richest man in the town.'

'My father's the richest man in Wales.'

'My father owns the world.'

And swopped gob-stoppers for slings, old knives for marbles, kite string for foreign stamps.

The lane was always the place to tell your secrets, if you did not have any you invented them: occasionally now I dream that I am turning out of school into the lane of confidences when I say to the boys of my class, 'At last, I have a real secret.'

'What is it? What is it?'

'I can fly.'

And when they do not believe me, I flap my arms and slowly leave the ground, only a few inches at first, then gaining air until I fly waving my cap level with the upper windows of the school, peering in until the mistress at the piano screams and the metronome falls to the ground and stops, and there is no more time.

And I fly over the trees and chimneys of my town, over the dockyards skimming the masts and funnels, over Inkerman Street, Sebastopol Street, and the street where all the women wear men's caps, over the trees of the everlasting park, where a brass band shakes the leaves and sends them showering down on to the nurses and the children, the cripples and the idlers, and the gardeners, and the shouting boys: over the yellow seashore, and the stone-chasing dogs, and the old men, and the singing sea.

The memories of childhood have no order, and no end.

Quite Early One Morning

Quite early one morning in the winter in Wales, by the sea that was lying down still and green as grass after a night of tar-black howling and rolling, I went out of the house, where I had come to stay for a cold unseasonable holiday, to see if it was raining still, if the outhouse had been blown away, potatoes, shears, rat-killer, shrimp-nets, and tins of rusty nails aloft on the wind, and if all the cliffs were left. It had been such a ferocious night that someone in the smoky shipped-pictured bar had said he could feel his tombstone shaking even though he was not dead, or at least was moving; but the morning shone as clear and calm as one always imagines to-morrow will shine.

The sun lit the sea town, not as a whole—from topmost down—reproving zinc-roofed chapel to empty but for rats and whispers grey warehouse on the harbour, but in separate bright pieces. There, the quay shouldering out, nobody on it now but the gulls and the capstans like small men in tubular trousers. Here, the roof of the police-station, black as a helmet, dry as a summons, sober as Sunday. There, the splashed church, with a cloud in the shape of a bell poised above it, ready to drift and ring. Here the chimneys of the pink-washed pub, the pub that was waiting for Saturday night as an over-jolly girl waits for sailors.

The town was not yet awake. The milkman lay still lost in the clangour and music of his Welsh-spoken dreams, the wish-fulfilled tenor voices more powerful than Caruso's, sweeter than Ben Davies's, thrilling past Cloth Hall and Manchester House up to the frosty hills. The town was not yet awake. Babies in upper bedrooms of salt-white houses dangling over water, or of bow-windowed villas squatting prim in neatly treed but unsteady hill streets, worried the light with their half in sleep cries. Miscellaneous retired sea captains emerged for a second from deeper waves than ever tossed their boats, then drowned again, going down down into a perhaps Mediterranean-blue cabin of sleep, rocked to the sea-beat of their ears. Landladies, shawled and bloused and aproned with sleep in the curtained, bombasined black of their once spare rooms, remember their loves, their bills, their visitors—dead, decamped, or buried in English deserts till the trumpet of next expensive August roused them again to the world of holiday rain, dismal cliff and sand seen through the weeping windows of front parlours, tasselled table-cloths, stuffed pheasants, ferns in pots, fading photographs of the bearded and censorious dead, autograph albums with a lock of limp and colourless beribboned hair lolling out between the thick black boards.

The town was not yet awake. Birds sang in eaves, bushes, trees, on telegraph wires, rails, fences, spars, and wet masts, not for love or joy, but to keep other birds away. The landlords in feathers disputed the right of even the flying light to descend and perch.

The town was not yet awake, and I walked through the streets like a stranger come out of the sea, shrugging off weed and wave and darkness with each step, or like an inquisitive shadow, determined to miss nothing—not the preliminary tremor in the throat of the dawn-saying cock or the first whirring nudge of arranged time in the belly of the alarm clock on the trinketed chest of drawers under the knitted text and the done-by-hand water-colours of Porthcawl or Trinidad.

I walked past the small sea-spying windows, behind whose trim curtains lay mild-mannered men and women not yet awake and, for all I could know, terrible and violent in their dreams. In the head of Miss Hughes, 'The Cosy,' clashed the cymbals of an eastern court. Eunuchs struck gongs the size of Bethesda Chapel. Sultans with voices fiercer than visiting preachers demanded a most un-Welsh dance. Everywhere there glowed and rayed the colours of the small, slate-grey woman's dreams, purple, magenta, ruby, sapphire, emerald, vermilion, honey. But I could not believe it. She knitted in her tidy sleep-world a beige woollen shroud with 'thou shalt not' on the bosom.

I could not imagine Cadwallader Davies the grocer in his near-to-waking dream, riding on horse-back, two-gunned and Cody-bold, through the cactus prairies. He added, he subtracted, he receipted, he filed a prodigious account with a candle dipped in dried egg.

What big seas of dreams ran in the Captain's sleep? Over what blue-whaled waves did he sail through a rainbow hail of flying-fishes to the music of Circe's swinish island? Do not let him be dreaming of dividends and bottled beer and onions.

Someone was snoring in one house. I counted ten savage and indignant grunts and groans like those of a pig in a model and mudless farm which ended with a window rattler, a wash-basin shaker, a trembler of tooth glasses, a waker of dormice. It thundered with me to the chapel railings, then brassily vanished.

The chapel stood grim and grey, telling the day there was to be no nonsense. The chapel was not asleep, it never cat-napped nor nodded nor closed its long cold eye. I left it telling the morning off and the sea-gull hung rebuked above it.

And climbing down again and up out of the town I heard the cocks crow from hidden farmyards, from old roosts above waves where fabulous sea-birds might sit and cry: 'Neptune!' And a far-away clock struck from another church in another village in another universe, though the wind blew the time away. And I walked in the timeless morning past a row of white cottages almost expecting that an ancient man with a great beard and an hour-glass and a scythe under his night-dressed arm might lean from the window and ask me the time. I would have told him: 'Arise old counter of the heart-beats of albatrosses, and wake the cavernous sleepers of the town to a dazzling new morning.' I would have told him: 'You unbelievable Father of Eva and Dai Adam, come out, old chicken, and stir up the winter morning with your spoon of a scythe.' I would have told him—I would have scampered like a scalded ghost over the cliffs and down to the bilingual sea.

Who lived in these cottages? I was a stranger to the sea town, fresh or stale from the city where I worked for my bread and butter wishing it were laver-bread and country salty butter yolk-yellow. Fishermen certainly; no painters but of boats; no man-dressed women with shooting-sticks and sketch-books and voices like macaws to paint the reluctant heads of critical and sturdy natives who posed by the pint against the chapel-dark sea which would be made more blue than the bay of Naples—though shallower.

I walked on to the cliff path again, the town behind and below waking up now so very slowly; I stopped and turned and looked. Smoke from one chimney—the cobbler's I thought, but from that distance it may have been the chimney of the retired male nurse who had come to live in Wales after many years successful wrestling with the mad rich of southern England. He was not liked. He measured you for a strait-jacket carefully with his eye; he saw you bounce from rubber walls like a sorbo ball. No behaviour surprised him. Many people of the town found it hard to resist leering at him suddenly around the corner, or convulsively dancing, or pointing with laughter and devilish good humour at invisible dog-fights merely to prove to him that they were normal.

Smoke from another chimney now. They were burning their last night's dreams. Up from a chimney came a long-haired wraith like an old politician. Someone had been dreaming of the Liberal Party. But no, the smoky figure wove, attentuated into a refined and precise grey comma. Someone had been dreaming of reading Charles Morgan. Oh! the town was waking now and I heard distinctly insistent over the slow-speaking sea the voices of the town blown up to me. And some of the voices said:

I am Miss May Hughes 'The Cosy,' a lonely lady,
Waiting in her house by the nasty sea,
Waiting for her husband and pretty baby
To come home at last from wherever they may be.

I am Captain Tiny Evans, my ship was the *Kidwelly*,
And Mrs Tiny Evans has been dead for many a year.
'Poor Captain Tiny all alone,' the neighbours whisper,
But I like it all alone and I hated her.

Clara Tawe Jenkins, 'Madam' they call me,
An old contralto with her dressing-gown on,
And I sit at the window and I sing to the sea,
For the sea does not notice that my voice has gone.

Parchedig Thomas Evans making morning tea,
Very weak tea, too, you mustn't waste a leaf.
Every morning making tea in my house by the sea,
I am troubled by one thing only, and that, belief.

Open the curtains, light the fire, what are servants for?
I am Mrs Ogmore Pritchard and I want another snooze.
Dust the china, feed the canary, sweep the drawing-
    room floor;
And before you let the sun in, mind he wipes his shoes.

I am only Mr Griffiths, very short-sighted, B.A., Aber.
As soon as I finish my egg I must shuffle off to school.
O patron saint of teachers, teach me to keep order,
And forget those words on the blackboard—'Griffiths
    Bat is a fool.'

Do you hear that whistling?—It's me, I am Phoebe,
The maid at the King's Head, and I am whistling like
    a bird.
Someone spilt a tin of pepper in the tea.
There's twenty for breakfast and I'm not going to say
    a word.

Thus some of the voices of a cliff-perched town at the far end of Wales moved out of sleep and darkness into the new-born, ancient, and ageless morning, moved and were lost.

Memories of Christmas

One Christmas was so much like another, in those years, around the sea-town corner now, and out of all sound except the distant speaking of the voices I sometimes hear a moment before sleep, that I can never remember whether it snowed for six days and six nights when I was twelve or whether it snowed for twelve days and twelve nights when I was six; or whether the ice broke and the skating grocer vanished like a snowman through a white trap-door on that same Christmas Day that the mince-pies finished Uncle Arnold and we tobogganed down the seaward hill, all the afternoon, on the best tea-tray, and Mrs Griffiths complained, and we threw a snowball at her niece, and my hands burned so, with the heat and the cold, when I held them in front of the fire, that I cried for twenty minutes and then had some jelly.

All the Christmases roll down the hill towards the Welsh-speaking sea, like a snowball growing whiter and bigger and rounder, like a cold and headlong moon bundling down the sky that was our street; and they stop at the rim of the ice-edged, fish-freezing waves, and I plunge my hands in the snow and bring out whatever I can find; holly or robins or pudding, squabbles and carols and oranges and tin whistles, and the fire in the front room, and bang go the crackers, and holy, holy, holy, ring the bells, and the glass bells shaking on the tree, and Mother Goose, and Struwelpeter—oh! the baby-burning flames and the clacking scissorman!—Billy Bunter and Black Beauty, Little Women and boys who have three helpings, Alice and Mrs Potter's badgers, penknives, teddy-bears—named after a Mr Theodore Bear, their inventor, or father, who died recently in the United States—mouth-organs, tin-soldiers, and blancmange, and Auntie Bessie playing 'Pop Goes the Weasel' and 'Nuts in May' and 'Oranges and Lemons' on the untuned piano in the parlour all through the thimble-hiding musical-chairing blind-man's-buffing party at the end of the never-to-be-forgotten day at the end of the unremembered year.

In goes my hand into that wool-white bell-tongued ball of holidays resting at the margin of the carol-singing sea, and out come Mrs Prothero and the firemen.

It was on the afternoon of the day of Christmas Eve, and I was in Mrs Prothero's garden, waiting for cats, with her son Jim. It was snowing. It was always snowing at Christmas; December, in my memory, is white as Lapland, though there were no reindeers. But there were cats. Patient, cold, and callous, our hands wrapped in socks, we waited to snowball the cats. Sleek and long as jaguars and terrible-whiskered, spitting and snarling they would slink and sidle over the white back-garden walls, and the lynx-eyed hunters, Jim and I, fur-capped and moccasined trappers from Hudson's Bay off Eversley Road, would hurl our deadly snowballs at the green of their eyes. The wise cats never appeared. We were so still, Eskimo-footed arctic marksmen in the muffling silence of the eternal snows—eternal, ever since Wednesday—that we never heard Mrs Prothero's first cry from her igloo at the bottom of the garden. Or, if we heard it at all, it was, to us, like the far-off challenge of our enemy and prey, the neighbour's Polar Cat. But soon the voice grew louder. 'Fire!' cried Mrs Prothero, and she beat the dinner-gong. And we ran down the garden, with the snowballs in our arms, towards the house, and smoke, indeed, was pouring out of the dining-room, and the gong was bombilating, and Mrs Prothero was announcing ruin like a town-crier in Pompeii. This was better than all the cats in Wales standing on the wall in a row. We bounded into the house, laden with snow-balls, and stopped at the open door of the smoke-filled room. Something was burning all right; perhaps it was Mr Prothero, who always slept there after midday dinner with a newspaper over his face; but he was standing in the middle of the room, saying 'A fine Christmas!' and smacking at the smoke with a slipper.

'Call the fire-brigade,' cried Mrs Prothero as she beat the gong.

'They won't be there,' said Mr Prothero, 'it's Christmas.'

There was no fire to be seen, only clouds of smoke and Mr Prothero standing in the middle of them, waving his slipper as though he were conducting.

'Do something,' he said.

And we threw all our snowballs into the smoke—I think we missed Mr Prothero—and ran out of the house to the telephone-box.

'Let's call the police as well,' Jim said.

'And the ambulance.'

'And Ernie Jenkins, he likes fires.'

But we only called the fire-brigade, and soon the fire-engine came and three tall men in helmets brought a hose into the house and Mr Prothero got out just in time before they turned it on. Nobody could have had a noisier Christmas Eve. And when the firemen turned off the hose and were standing in the wet and smoky room, Jim's aunt, Miss Prothero, came downstairs and peered in at them. Jim and I waited, very quietly, to hear what she would say to them. She said the right thing, always. She looked at the three tall firemen in their shining helmets, standing among the smoke and cinders and dissolving snowballs, and she said: 'Would you like something to read?'

Now out of that bright white snowball of Christmas gone comes the stocking, the stocking of stockings, that hung at the foot of the bed with the arm of a golliwog dangling over the top and small bells ringing in the toes. There was a company, gallant and scarlet but never nice to taste though I always tried when very young, of belted and busbied and musketed lead soldiers so soon to lose their heads and legs in the wars on the kitchen table after the tea-things, the mince-pies, and the cakes that I helped to make by stoning the raisins and eating them, had been cleared away; and a bag of moist and many-coloured jelly-babies and a folded flag and a false nose and a tram-conductor's cap and a machine that punched tickets and rang a bell; never a catapult; once, by a mistake that no one could explain, a little hatchet; and a rubber buffalo, or it may have been a horse, with a yellow head and haphazard legs; and a celluloid duck that made, when you pressed it, a most unducklike noise, a mewing moo that an ambitious cat might make who wishes to be a cow; and a painting-book in which I could make the grass, the trees, the sea, and the animals any colour I pleased: and still the dazzling sky-blue sheep are grazing in the red field under a flight of rainbow-beaked and pea-green birds.

Christmas morning was always over before you could

say Jack Frost. And look! suddenly the pudding was burning! Bang the gong and call the fire-brigade and the book-loving firemen! Someone found the silver three-penny-bit with a currant on it; and the someone was always Uncle Arnold. The motto in my cracker read:

Let's all have fun this Christmas Day,
Let's play and sing and shout hooray!

and the grown-ups turned their eyes towards the ceiling, and Auntie Bessie, who had already been frightened, twice, by a clockwork mouse, whimpered at the side-board and had some elderberry wine. And someone put a glass bowl full of nuts on the littered table, and my uncle said, as he said once every year: 'I've got a shoe-nut here. Fetch me a shoe-horn to open it, boy.'

And dinner was ended.

And I remember that on the afternoon of Christmas Day, when the others sat around the fire and told each other that this was nothing, no, nothing, to the great snowbound and turkey-proud yule-log-crackling holly-berry-bedizined and kissing-under-the-mistletoe Christmas when *they* were children, I would go out, school-capped and gloved and mufflered, with my bright new boots squeaking, into the white world on to the seaward hill, to call on Jim and Dan and Jack and to walk with them through the silent snowscape of our town.

We went padding through the streets, leaving huge deep footprints in the snow, on the hidden pavements.

'I bet people'll think there's been hippoes.'

'What would you do if you saw a hippo coming down Terrace Road?'

'I'd go like this, bang! I'd throw him over the

railings and roll him down the hill and then I'd tickle him under the ear and he'd wag his tail . . .'

'What would you do if you saw *two* hippoes . . .?'

Iron-flanked and bellowing he-hippoes clanked and blundered and battered through the scudding snow towards us as we passed by Mr Daniel's house.

'Let's post Mr Daniel a snowball through his letter-box.'

'Let's write things in the snow.'

'Let's write "Mr Daniel looks like a spaniel" all over his lawn.'

'Look,' Jack said, 'I'm eating snow-pie.'

'What's it taste like?'

'Like snow-pie,' Jack said.

Or we walked on the white shore.

'Can the fishes see it's snowing?'

'They think it's the sky falling down.'

The silent one-clouded heavens drifted on to the sea.

'All the old dogs have gone.'

Dogs of a hundred mingled makes yapped in the summer at the sea-rim and yelped at the trespassing mountains of the waves.

'I bet St Bernards would like it now.'

And we were snowblind travellers lost on the north hills, and the great dewlapped dogs, with brandy-flasks round their necks, ambled and shambled up to us, baying 'Excelsior.'

We returned home through the desolate poor sea-facing streets where only a few children fumbled with bare red fingers in the thick wheel-rutted snow and cat-called after us, their voices fading away, as we trudged uphill, into the cries of the dock-birds and the hooters of ships out in the white and whirling bay.

Bring out the tall tales now that we told by the fire as we roasted chestnuts and the gaslight bubbled low. Ghosts with their heads under their arms trailed their chains and said 'whooo' like owls in the long nights when I dared not look over my shoulder; wild beasts lurked in the cubby-hole under the stairs where the gas-meter ticked. 'Once upon a time,' Jim said, 'there were three boys, just like us, who got lost in the dark in the snow, near Bethesda Chapel, and this is what happened to them. . . .' It was the most dreadful happening I had ever heard.

And I remember that we went singing carols once, a night or two before Christmas Eve, when there wasn't the shaving of a moon to light the secret, white-flying streets. At the end of a long road was a drive that led to a large house, and we stumbled up the darkness of the drive that night, each one of us afraid, each one holding a stone in his hand in case, and all of us too brave to say a word. The wind made through the drive-trees noises as of old and unpleasant and maybe web-footed men wheezing in caves. We reached the black bulk of the house.

'What shall we give them?' Dan whispered.

'"Hark the Herald"? "Christmas comes but Once a Year"?'

'No,' Jack said: 'We'll sing "Good King Wenceslas." I'll count three.'

One, two, three, and we began to sing, our voices high and seemingly distant in the snow-felted darkness round the house that was occupied by nobody we knew. We stood close together, near the dark door.

> Good King Wenceslas looked out
> On the Feast of Stephen.

And then a small, dry voice, like the voice of someone who has not spoken for a long time, suddenly joined our singing: a small, dry voice from the other side of the door: a small, dry voice through the keyhole. And when we stopped running we were outside *our* house; the front room was lovely and bright; the gramophone was playing; we saw the red and white balloons hanging from the gas-bracket; uncles and aunts sat by the fire; I thought I smelt our supper being fried in the kitchen. Everything was good again, and Christmas shone through all the familiar town.

'Perhaps it was a ghost,' Jim said.

'Perhaps it was trolls,' Dan said, who was always reading.

'Let's go in and see if there's any jelly left,' Jack said. And we did that.

Holiday Memory

August Bank Holiday. A tune on an ice-cream cornet. A slap of sea and a tickle of sand. A fanfare of sunshades opening. A wince and whinny of bathers dancing into deceptive water. A tuck of dresses. A rolling of trousers. A compromise of paddlers. A sunburn of girls and a lark of boys. A silent hullabaloo of balloons.

I remember the sea telling lies in a shell held to my ear for a whole harmonious, hollow minute by a small, wet girl in an enormous bathing-suit marked 'Corporation Property.'

I remember sharing the last of my moist buns with a boy and a lion. Tawny and savage, with cruel nails and capacious mouth, the little boy tore and devoured. Wild as seed-cake, ferocious as a hearth-rug, the depressed and verminous lion nibbled like a mouse at his half a bun, and hiccupped in the sad dusk of his cage.

I remember a man like an alderman or a bailiff, bowlered and collarless, with a bag of monkey-nuts in his hand, crying 'Ride 'em, cowboy!' time and again as he whirled in his chairoplane giddily above the upturned laughing faces of the town girls bold as brass and the boys with padded shoulders and shoes sharp as knives; and the monkey-nuts flew through the air like salty hail.

Children all day capered or squealed by the glazed or bashing sea, and the steam-organ wheezed its waltzes in the threadbare playground and the waste lot, where the dodgems dodged, behind the pickle factory.

And mothers loudly warned their proud pink daughters or sons to put that jellyfish down; and fathers spread newspapers over their faces; and sand-fleas hopped on the picnic lettuce; and someone had forgotten the salt.

In those always radiant, rainless, lazily rowdy and sky-blue summers departed, I remember August Monday from the rising of the sun over the stained and royal town to the husky hushing of the roundabout music and the dowsing of the naphtha jets in the seaside fair: from bubble-and-squeak to the last of the sandy sandwiches.

There was no need, that holiday morning, for the sluggardly boys to be shouted down to breakfast; out of their jumbled beds they tumbled, scrambled into their rumpled clothes; quickly at the bath-room basin they catlicked their hands and faces, but never forgot to run the water loud and long as though they washed like colliers; in front of the cracked looking-glass bordered with cigarette-cards, in their treasure-trove bedrooms, they whisked a gap-tooth comb through their surly hair; and with shining cheeks and noses and tide-marked necks, they took the stairs three at a time.

But for all their scramble and scamper, clamour on the landing, catlick and toothbrush flick, hair-whisk and stair-jump, their sisters were always there before them. Up with the lady lark, they had prinked and frizzed and hot-ironed; and smug in their blossoming dresses, ribboned for the sun, in gym-shoes white as the blanco'd snow, neat and silly with doilies and tomatoes they helped in the higgledy kitchen. They were calm; they were virtuous; they had washed their necks; they did not romp, or fidget; and only the smallest sister put out her tongue at the noisy boys.

And the woman who lived next door came into the

kitchen and said that her mother, an ancient uncertain body who wore a hat with cherries, was having 'one of her days' and had insisted, that very holiday morning, in carrying all the way to the tram-stop a photograph album and the cut-glass fruit-bowl from the front room.

This was the morning when father, mending one hole in the thermos-flask, made three; when the sun declared war on the butter, and the butter ran; when dogs, with all the sweet-binned backyards to wag and sniff and bicker in, chased their tails in the jostling kitchen, worried sandshoes, snapped at flies, writhed between legs, scratched among towels, sat smiling on hampers.

And if you could have listened at some of the open doors of some of the houses in the street you might have heard:

'Uncle Owen says he can't find the bottle-opener . . .'

'Has he looked under the hallstand?'

'Willy's cut his finger . . .'

'Got your spade?'

'If somebody doesn't kill that dog . . .'

'Uncle Owen says why should the bottle-opener be under the hall-stand?'

'Never again, never again . . .'

'I know I put the pepper somewhere . . .'

'Willy's bleeding . . .'

'Look, there's a bootlace in my bucket . . .'

'Oh come *on*, come on . . .'

'Let's have a look at the bootlace in your bucket . . .'

'If I lay my hands on that dog . . .'

'Uncle Owen's found the bottle-opener . . .'

'Willy's bleeding over the cheese . . .'

And the trams that hissed like ganders took us all to the beautiful beach.

There was cricket on the sand, and sand in the sponge cake, sand-flies in the watercress, and foolish, mulish, religious donkeys on the unwilling trot. Girls undressed in slipping tents of propriety; under invisible umbrellas, stout ladies dressed for the male and immoral sea. Little naked navvies dug canals; children with spades and no ambition built fleeting castles; wispy young men, outside the bathing-huts, whistled at substantial young women and dogs who desired thrown stones more than the bones of elephants. Recalcitrant uncles huddled over luke ale in the tiger-striped marquees. Mothers in black, like wobbling mountains, gasped under the discarded dresses of daughters who shrilly braved the goblin waves. And fathers, in the once-a-year sun, took fifty winks. Oh, think of all the fifty winks along the paper-bagged sand.

Liquorice allsorts, and Welsh hearts, were melting, and the sticks of rock, that we all sucked, were like barbers' poles made of rhubarb.

In the distance, surrounded by disappointed theoreticians and an ironmonger with a drum, a cross man on an orange-box shouted that holidays were wrong.

And the waves rolled in, with rubber ducks and clerks upon them.

I remember the patient, laborious, and enamouring hobby, or profession, of burying relatives in sand.

I remember the princely pastime of pouring sand, from cupped hands or buckets, down collars and tops of dresses; the shriek, the shake, the slap.

I can remember the boy by himself, the beachcombing lone-wolf, hungrily waiting at the edge of family cricket; the friendless fielder, the boy uninvited to bat or to tea.

I remember the smell of sea and seaweed, wet flesh,

wet hair, wet bathing-dresses, the warm smell as of a rabbity field after rain, the smell of pop and splashed sunshades and toffee, the stable-and-straw smell of hot, tossed, tumbled, dug, and trodden sand, the swill-and-gaslamp smell of Saturday night, though the sun shone strong, from the bellying beer-tents, the smell of the vinegar on shelled cockles, winkle-smell, shrimp-smell, the dripping-oily backstreet winter-smell of chips in newspapers, the smell of ships from the sun-dazed docks round the corner of the sand-hills, the smell of the known and paddled-in sea moving, full of the drowned and herrings, out and away and beyond and further still towards the antipodes that hung their koala-bears and Maoris, kangaroos, and boomerangs, upside down over the backs of the stars.

And the noise of pummelling Punch, and Judy falling, and a clock tolling or telling no time in the tenantless town; now and again a bell from a lost tower or a train on the lines behind us clearing its throat, and always the hopeless, ravenous swearing and pleading of the gulls, donkey-bray and hawker-cry, harmonicas and toy trumpets, shouting and laughing and singing, hooting of tugs and tramps, the clip of the chair-attendant's puncher, the motor-boat coughing in the bay, and the same hymn and washing of the sea that was heard in the Bible.

'If it could only just, if it could only just?' your lips said again and again as you scooped, in the hob-hot sand, dungeons, garages, torture-chambers, train tunnels, arsenals, hangars for zeppelins, witches' kitchens, vampires' parlours, smugglers' cellars, trolls' grog-shops, sewers, under a ponderous and cracking castle, 'If it could only just be like this for ever and ever amen.' August Monday all over the earth, from Mumbles where the aunties grew like ladies on a seaside tree to brown, bear-hugging Henty-land and the turtled Ballantyne Islands.

'Could donkeys go on the ice?'

'Only if they got snowshoes.'

We snowshoed a meek, complaining donkey and galloped him off in the wake of the ten-foot-tall and Atlas-muscled Mounties, rifled and pemmicanned, who always, in the white Gold Rush wastes, got their black-oathed-and-bearded Man.

'Are there donkeys on desert islands?'

'Only sort-of donkeys.'

'What d'you mean, sort-of donkeys?'

'Native donkeys. They hunt things on them!'

'Sort-of walruses and seals and things?'

'Donkeys can't swim!'

'These donkeys can. They swim like whales, they swim like anything, they swim like——'

'Liar.'

'Liar yourself.'

And two small boys fought fiercely and silently in the sand, rolling together in a ball of legs and bottoms.

Then they went and saw the pierrots, or bought vanilla ices.

Lolling or larrikin that unsoiled, boiling beauty of a common day, great gods with their braces over their vests sang, spat pips, puffed smoke at wasps, gulped and ogled, forgot the rent, embraced, posed for the dicky-bird, were coarse, had rainbow-coloured armpits, winked, belched, blamed the radishes, looked at Ilfracombe, played hymns on paper-and-comb, peeled bananas, scratched, found seaweed in their panamas, blew up paper-bags and banged them, wished for nothing.

But over all the beautiful beach I remember most the children playing, boys and girls tumbling, moving jewels, who might never be happy again. And 'happy as a sandboy' is true as the heat of the sun.

Dusk came down; or grew up out of the sands and the sea; or curled around us from the calling docks and the bloodily smoking sun. The day was done, the sands brushed and ruffled suddenly with a sea-broom of cold wind.

And we gathered together all the spades and buckets and towels, empty hampers and bottles, umbrellas and fish-frails, bats and balls and knitting, and went—oh, listen, Dad!—to the fair in the dusk on the bald seaside field.

Fairs were no good in the day; then they were shoddy and tired; the voices of hoop-la girls were crimped as elocutionists; no cannon-ball could shake the roosting coco-nuts; the gondolas mechanically repeated their sober lurch; the Wall of Death was safe as a governess cart; the wooden animals were waiting for the night.

But in the night, the hoop-la girls, like operatic crows, croaked at the coming moon; whizz, whirl, and ten for a tanner, the coco-nuts rained from their sawdust like grouse from the Highland sky; tipsy the griffin-prowed gondolas weaved on dizzy rails and the Wall of Death was a spinning rim of ruin, and the neighing wooden horses took, to a haunting hunting tune, a thousand Becher's Brooks as easily and breezily as hooved swallows.

Approaching, at dusk, the fair-field from the beach, we scorched and gritty boys heard above the belabouring of the batherless sea the siren voices of the raucous, horsy barkers.

'Roll up, roll up!'

In her tent and her rolls of flesh the Fattest Woman in the World sat sewing her winter frock, another tent, and fixed her little eyes, blackcurrants in blancmange, on the skeletons who filed and sniggered by.

'Roll up, roll up, roll up to see the Largest Rat on Earth, the Rover or Bonzo of vermin.'

Here scampered the smallest pony, like a Shetland shrew. And here 'The Most Intelligent Fleas,' trained, reined, bridled, and bitted, minutely cavorted in their glass corral.

Round galleries and shies and stalls, pennies were burning holes in a hundred pockets.

Pale young men with larded hair and Valentino-black side-whiskers, fags stuck to their lower lips, squinted along their swivel-sighted rifles and aimed at ping-pong balls dancing on fountains.

In knife-creased, silver-grey, skirt-like Oxford bags, and a sleeveless, scarlet, zip-fastened shirt with yellow horizontal stripes, a collier at the strength-machine spat on his hands, raised the hammer, and brought it Thor-ing down. The bell rang for Blaina.

Outside his booth stood a bitten-eared and barndoor-chested pug with a nose like a twisted swede and hair that started from his eyebrows and three teeth yellow as a camel's inviting any sportsman to a sudden and sickening basting in the sandy ring or a quid if he lasted a round; and, wiry, cocky, bow-legged, coal-scarred, boozed, sportsmen by the dozen strutted in and reeled out; and still those three teeth remained, chipped and camel-yellow in the bored, teak face.

Draggled and stout-wanting mothers, with haphazard hats, hostile hatpins, buns awry, bursting bags, and children at their skirts like pop-filled and jam-smeared limpets, screamed before distorting mirrors, at their suddenly tapering or tubular bodies and huge ballooning heads, and the children gaily bellowed at their own reflected bogies withering and bulging in the glass.

Old men, smelling of Milford Haven in the rain, shuffled, badgering and cadging, round the edges of the swaggering crowd, their only wares a handful of damp confetti.

A daring dash of schoolboys, safely, shoulder to shoulder, with their father's trilbies cocked at a desperate angle over one eye, winked at and whistled after the procession past the swings of two girls arm-in-arm: always one pert and pretty, and always one with glasses.

Girls in skulled and cross-boned tunnels shrieked, and were comforted.

Young men, heroic after pints, stood up on the flying chairoplanes, tousled, crimson, and against the rules.

Jaunty girls gave sailors sauce.

All the fun of the fair in the hot, bubbling night. The Man in the sand-yellow moon over the hurdy of gurdies. The swing-boats swimming to and fro like slices of the moon. Dragons and hippogriffs at the prows of the gondolas breathing fire and Sousa. Midnight roundabout riders tantivying under the fairy-lights, huntsmen on billygoats and zebras hallooing under a circle of glow-worms.

And as we climbed home, up the gas-lit hill, to the still homes over the mumbling bay, we heard the music die and the voices drift like sand. And we saw the lights of the fair fade. And, at the far end of the seaside field, they lit their lamps, one by one, in the caravans.

How to begin a Story

The way to begin a story depends not so much upon what you mean by a story as upon the story itself and the public for which it is intended. That this goes without saying need in no way deter me from saying it: these are notes in the margin of a never-to-be-written treatise and are free as the London air, though not so smutty.

It would, for example, be wrong, however pleasant, to begin a story for *Little Tim's Weekly* in the style of a sentimentally savage, gauchely cynical, American underworld novel salted with sex-slang, peppered with lead, sugared with stiffs and stiff with cigars and sugars: the kind of novel beneath whose hard and sinister shell lurks no embryonic bird of prey, great Chicago auk or fabulous Brooklyn roc, but a backward, shy and shabby backwood sparrow twittering for crumbs and buddies. Those flash, brash, cigar-mashing floozy-flayers and anti-social bad babies who, in recent gangster-films, confess, at some Ufa-lighted moment in abattoir, railway-siding, or condemned cell, that they have always been kinda unwanted and lonesome, even back in mid-western little Bloodville, and that it all began when their dipsomaniac second stepmothers put them on the fire for saying their prayers—these psychopathic gorillas coked to the gills have no place in Little Tim's cosmography, however much Little Tim would appreciate it, and the writer of children's stories should never, in any circumstances, emotional or atomic, begin with an expletive-packed and monosyllabic description of a raid by the vice-squad on a clip-joint for retired rod-men. It is legitimate to begin a children's story with a conversation between rats; but only between certain kinds of rats.

Neither should the writer of a story intended to command a steady, unsensational provincial sale, and concerning the birth, education, financial ups and downs, marriage, separations, and deaths of five generations of a family of Lancashire cotton-weavers, begin with, say, the Joyceian interior monologue of a moronic haberdasher trapped in a lift full of moths, or with a twee scene, in Hopskipandjump Town or Eiderdown Land, between Gruffums, the Lion, and Hold, that Tiger.

The man who begins a story for a girl's popular weekly—'Myrtle's' or 'Pam's,' or maybe it is 'Greta's' now, or 'Ingrid's'—with a subtle analysis of the state of mind of a neurotic young man of letters about to meet a phobia, socially, in a disused Nissen-hut, will never make the grade and is doomed to perpetual immurement in magazines with a circulation of seventeen poets and a woman who once met Kafka's aunt.

Now let us consider, most briefly, just a very few of the many favourite ways of beginning stories, and see if we can put a little new life into them.

School-stories first: not the dull ones about the repressions and urges of sensitive plants and backward sons, and the first dawning of love and Shelley on the awakening mind, but the good, or bad, old stories which are all about tea and muffins in the cosy study, midnight spreads by candlelight in the ill-patrolled dormitory, escapes by knotted sheets to out-of-bound circuses or fairs, the ruthless ragging and baiting of unpopular masters and impecunious buffoons, the expulsion of cads for smoking in the fives-court—poor little sallow Maltravers with the dark rings already under his *roué*'s eyes—and all the trivial tribal warfares of fantastic and ageless boys.

The onomatopoeic, gemmed and magnetic, time-honoured opening cannot be bettered:

'Leggo!'

'Geroff!'

'Yaroo!'

And then, of course:

'These stentorian cries echoed down the corridor of the Upper Shell.'

The novice should begin every school story with exactly those words.

In the next sentence he must introduce his principal characters, a bunch of bold, breathless, exclamatory, ink-stained, beastly, Dickensian-surnamed boys with their caps awry, their lines undone, pets in their desks, paper-pellets in their pockets, and barbarous though innocuous oaths on their unrazored lips.

But let us introduce a new element:

'Leggo!'

'Geroff!'

'Yaroo!'

'These stentorian cries echoed down the corridor of the Upper Shell as Tom Happy and his inseparables, known to all Owlhurst as the "Filthy Five," lurched arm-in-arm out of Mrs Motherwell's fully licensed tuckshop.'

There you have a beginning at once conventional and startling. The reader is at your mercy. And you can continue, within the accepted framework and using only the loudest, minutest, and most formal vocabulary, to describe such goings-on as the formation, by Tom Happy, of the Owlhurst Suicide Club and the setting-up of a hookah in the boothole.

Then there is the story of rural life. I don't mean the depressing tale, told through four interminable seasons, of rugged toil and weather-beaten love on an isolated farm of that part of Sussex where you can't hear the thrushes for the noise of typewriters; nor the earthy, middenish record, stuffed with nature lore and agricultural information, studded—if that is the word—with all too precise observations of animal behaviour, whiskered with 'characters,' riddled with unintelligible snatches of folk-verse and altogether jocular as a boot, of how a middle-aged literary man 'discovered' the country and his soul, price eight and six. No; I mean the kind of story set in a small, lunatic area of Wessex, full of saintly or reprehensible vicars, wanton maidens, biblical sextons, and old men called Parsnip or Dottle.

Let us imagine a typical beginning:

'Mr Beetroot stood on a hill overlooking the village of Upper Story. He saw that there was something wrong in it. Mr Beetroot was a retired mole-trapper. He had retired because he had trapped all the moles. It was a fine winter's morning, and there were little clouds in the sky like molehills. Mr Beetroot caught a rabbit, taught it the alphabet, let it go, and walked slowly down the hill.'

There we have firmly fixed the location and mood of the story, and have become well, if briefly, acquainted with Mr Beetroot, a lover of animals and addicted to animal education.

The common reader—legendary cretin—now knows what is coming to him: Mr Beetroot, that cracked though cosmic symbol of something or other, will, in the nutty village, with dialect, oafs, and potted sermons, conduct his investigation into unreal rural life. Everyone, in this sophisticatedly contrived bucolic morality, has his or her obsession: Minnie Wurzel wants only the vicar; the vicar, the Reverend Nut, wants only the ghost of William Cowper to come into his brown study and read him 'The Task'; the Sexton wants worms; worms want the vicar. Lambkins, on those impossible hills, frolic, gambol, and are sheepish under the all-seeing eye of Uncle Teapot, the Celestial Tinker. Cruel farmers persecute old cowherds called Crumpet, who talk, all day long, to cows; cows, tired of vaccine-talk in which they can have no part, gore, in a female manner, the aged relatives of cruel farmers; it is all very cosy in Upper Story. But so the reader—cretinous legend—thinks.

The beginner, beginning a story of this kind, would be wise to . . .

I see there is little, or no, time to continue my instructional essay on 'How to Begin a Story.' How to 'End a Story' is, of course, a different matter. . . . *One* way of ending a story is:

ANNOUNCER: That was Dylan Thomas talking about 'How to Begin a Story.'

The Crumbs of One Man's Year

Slung as though in a hammock, or a lull, between one Christmas for ever over and a New Year nearing full of relentless surprises, waywardly and gladly I pry back at those wizening twelve months and see only a waltzing snippet of the tipsy-turvy times, flickers of vistas, flashes of queer fishes, patches and chequers of a bard's-eye view.

Of what is coming in the New Year I know nothing, except that all that is certain will come like thunderclaps or like comets in the shape of four-leaved clovers, and that all that is unforeseen will appear with the certainty of the sun who every morning shakes a leg in the sky; and of what has gone I know only shilly-shally snatches and freckled plaids, flecks and dabs, dazzle and froth; a simple second caught in coursing snow-light, an instant, gay or sorry, struck motionless in the curve of flight like a bird or a scythe; the spindrift leaf and stray-paper whirl, canter, quarrel, and people-chase of everybody's street; suddenly the way the grotesque wind slashes and freezes at a corner the clothes of a passer-by so that she stays remembered, cold and still until the world like a night-light in a nursery goes out; and a waddling couple of the small occurrences, comic as ducks, that quack their way through our calamitous days; whits and dots and tittles.

'Look back, back,' the big voices clarion, 'look back at the black colossal year,' while the rich music fanfares and dead-marches.

I can give you only a scattering of some of the crumbs of one man's year; and the penny music whistles.

Any memory, of the long, revolving year, will do, to begin with.

I was walking, one afternoon in August, along a river-bank, thinking the same thoughts that I always think when I walk along a river-bank in August. As I was walking, I was thinking—now it is August and I am walking along a river-bank. I do not think I was thinking of anything else. I should have been thinking of what I should have been doing, but I was thinking only of what I was doing then and it was all right: it was good, and ordinary, and slow, and idle, and old, and sure, and what I was doing I could have been doing a thousand years before, had I been alive then and myself or any other man. You could have thought the river was ringing—almost you could hear the green, rapid bells sing in it: it could have been the River Elusina, 'that dances at the noise of Musick, for with Musick it bubbles, dances and growes sandy, and so continues till the musick ceases . . .' or it could have been the river 'in Judea that runs swiftly all the six dayes of the week, and stands still and rests all their Sabbath.' There were trees blowing, standing still, growing, knowing, whose names I never knew. (Once, indeed, with a friend I wrote a poem beginning, 'All trees are oaks, except fir-trees.') There were birds being busy, or sleep-flying, in the sky. (The poem had continued: 'All birds are robins, except crows, or rooks.') Nature was doing what it was doing, and thinking just that. And I was walking and thinking that I was walking, and for August it was not such a cold day. And then I saw, drifting along the water, a piece of paper, and I thought: Something wonderful may be written on this paper. I was alone on the gooseberry earth, or alone for two green miles, and a message drifted towards me on that tabby-coloured water that ran through the middle of the cow-patched, mooing fields. It was a message from multitudinous nowhere to my solitary self. I put out my stick and caught the piece of paper and held it close to the river-bank. It was a page torn from a very old periodical. That I could see. I leant over and read, through water, the message on the rippling page. I made out, with difficulty, only one sentence: it commemorated the fact that, over a hundred years ago, a man in Worcester had, for a bet, eaten, at one sitting, fifty-two pounds of plums.

And any other memory, of the long evolving year, will do, to go on with.

Here now, to my memory, come peaceful blitz and pieces of the Fifth of November, guys in the streets and forks in the sky, when Catherine-wheels and Jacky-jumps and good bombs burst in the blistered areas. The rockets are few but they star between roofs and up to the wall of the warless night. 'A penny for the Guy?' 'No, that's my father.' The great joke brocks and sizzles. Sirius explodes in the backyard by the shelter. Timorous ladies sit in their back-rooms, with the eighth programme on very loud. Retiring men snarl under their blankets. In the unkempt-gardens of the very rich, the second butler lights a squib. In everybody's street the fearless children shout, under the little, homely raids. But I was standing on a signalling country hill where they fed a hungry bonfire Guy with brushwood, sticks, and cracker-jacks; the bonfire Guy whooped for more; small sulphurous puddings banged in his burning belly, and his thorned hair caught. He lurched, and made common noises. He was a long time dying on the hill over the starlit fields where the tabby river, without a message, ran on, with bells and trout and tins and bangles and literature and cats in it, to the sea never out of sound.

And on one occasion, in this long dissolving year, I remember that I boarded a London bus from a district I have forgotten, and where I certainly could have been up to little good, to an appointment that I did not want to keep.

It was a shooting green spring morning, nimble and crocus, with all the young women treading on naked flower-stalks, the metropolitan sward, swinging their milk-pail handbags, gentle, fickle, inviting, accessible, forgiving each robustly abandoned gesture of salutation before it was made or imagined, assenting, as they revelled demurely towards the manicure *salon* or the typewriting office, to all the ardent unspoken endearments of shaggy strangers and the winks and pipes of clovenfooted sandwichmen. The sun shrilled, the buses gambolled, policemen and daffodils bowed in the breeze that tasted of buttermilk. Delicate carousal plashed and babbled from the public-houses which were not yet open. I felt like a young god. I removed my collar-studs and opened my shirt. I tossed back my hair. There was an aviary in my heart, but without any owls or eagles. My cheeks were cherried warm, I smelt, I thought, of sea-pinks. To the sound of madrigals sung by slim sopranos in waterfalled valleys where I was the only tenor, I leapt on to a bus. The bus was full. Carefree, open-collared, my eyes alight, my veins full of the spring as a dancer's shoes should be full of champagne, I stood, in love and at ease and always young, on the packed lower deck. And a man of exactly my own age —or perhaps he was a little older—got up and offered me his seat. He said, in a respectful voice, as though to an old justice of the peace, 'Please, won't you take my seat?' and then he added—'Sir.'

How many variegations of inconsiderable defeats and disillusionments I have forgotten! How many shades and shapes from the polychromatic zebra house! How many Joseph-coats I have left uncalled-for in the Gentlemen's Cloakrooms of the year!

And one man's year is like the country of a cloud, mapped on the sky, that soon will vanish into the watery, ordered wastes, into the spinning rule, into the dark which is light. Now the cloud is flying, very slowly, out of sight, and I can remember of all that voyaging geography, no palaced morning hills or huge plush valleys in the downing sun, forests simmering with birds, stagged moors, merry legendary meadowland, bullish plains, but only—the street near Waterloo station where a small boy, wearing cut-down khaki and a steel helmet, pushed a pram full of firewood and shouted, in a dispassionate voice, after each passer-by: 'Where's your tail?'

The estuary pool under the collapsed castle, where the July children rolled together in original mud, shrieking and yawping, and low life, long before newts, twitched on their hands.

The crisp path through the field in this December snow, in the deep dark, where we trod the buried grass like ghosts on dry toast.

The single-line run along the spring-green river-bank where water-voles went Indian file to work, and where the young impatient voles, in their sleek vests, always in a hurry, jumped over the threadbare backs of the old ones.

The razor-scarred back-street café bar where a man

with cut cheeks and chewed ears, huskily and furiously complained, over tarry tea, that the new baby panda in the zoo was not floodlit.

The gully sands in March, under the flayed and flailing cliff-top trees, when the wind played old Harry, or old Thomas, with me, and cormorants, far off, sped like motor-boats across the bay, as I weaved towards the toppling town and the black, loud *Lion* where the cat, who purred like a fire, looked out of two cinders at the gently swilling retired sea-captains in the snug-as-a-bug back bar.

And the basement kitchen in nipping February, with napkins on the line slung across from door to chocka-block corner, and a bicycle by the larder very much down at wheels, and hats and toy-engines and bottles and spanners on the broken rocking-chair, and billowing papers and half-finished crosswords stacked on the radio always turned full tilt, and the fire smoking, and onions peeling, and chips always spitting on the stove, and small men in their overcoats talking of self-discipline and the ascetic life until the air grew woodbine-blue and the clock choked and the traffic died.

And then the moment of a night in that cavorting spring, rare and unforgettable as a bicycle-clip found in the middle of the desert. The lane was long and soused and dark that led to the house I helped to fill and bedraggle.

'Who's left this in this corner?'

'What, where?'

'Here, this.'

A doll's arm, the chitterlings of a clock, a saucepan full of hatbands.

The lane was rutted as though by bosky watercarts,

and so dark you couldn't see your front in spite of you. Rain barrelled down. On one side you couldn't hear the deer that lived there, and on the other side—voices began to whisper, muffled in the midnight sack. A man's voice and a woman's voice. 'Lovers,' I said to myself. For at night the heart comes out, like a cat on the tiles. Discourteously I shone my torch. There, in the thick rain, a young man and a young woman stood, very close together, near the hedge that whirred in the wind. And a yard from them, another young man sat staidly, on the grass verge, holding an open book from which he appeared to read. And in the very rutted and puddly middle of the lane, two dogs were fighting, with brutish concentration and in absolute silence.

The Festival Exhibition, 1951

The extent of the site of the exhibition on the South Bank of the Thames in the heart of London is four and a half acres. There are twenty-two pavilions in the exhibition, and thirteen restaurants, cafés, bars, and buffets.

Some people visit the twenty-two pavilions first, then glazed and crippled, windless, rudderless, and a little out of their minds, teeter, weeping, to one of the thirteen restaurants, cafés, bars, and buffets to find it packed to the dazzlingly painted and, possibly, levitating doors.

Other people visit all thirteen restaurants, cafés, bars, and buffets before attacking the pavilions, and rarely get further than the Dome of Discovery, which they find confusing, full, as it is, of totem poles, real dogs in snow, locusts, stars, the sun, the moon, things bubbling, thunder and lightning machines, chemical and physical surprises. And some never return.

Most people who wish, at the beginning, anyway, to make sense of the exhibition, follow the course indicated in the official guide-book—a series of conflicting arrows which lead many visitors who cannot understand these things slap-splash into the Thames—and work their way dutifully right through the land of Britain, the glaciers of twenty thousand years ago, and the inferno of blown desert sand which is now Birmingham, out at last into the Pavilion of Health—where, perhaps, they stop for an envious moment at the sign that says 'Euthanasia'—and on to the netted and capstaned, bollarded, buoyed, sea-shelled, pebbly beautiful seaside of summer childhood gone.

And other visitors begin, of course, at the end. They are the people without whom the exhibition could not exist, nor the country it trombones and floats in with its lions and unicorns made of ears of wheat, its birds that sing to the push of a button, its flaming water, and its raspberry fountains. They are the suspicious people over whose eyes no coloured Festival wool can possibly be pulled, the great undiddleable; they are the women who 'will not queue on any account' and who smuggle in dyspeptic dogs; the strangely calculating men who think that the last pavilion must be first because it is number twenty-two; the people who believe they are somewhere else, and never find out they are not; sharp people who have been there before, who know the ropes, who chuckle to their country cousins: 'You get double your money's worth this way'; vaguely persecuted people, always losing their gloves, who know that the only way they could *ever* get around would be to begin at the end, which they do not want to; people of militant individuality who proclaim their right, as Englishmen, to look at the damfool place however they willynilly will; people nervously affected by all such occasions, who want to know only, 'Where's the place?'; timid people who want to be as far from the skylon as possible, because 'you never know'; foreigners, who have been directed this way by a school of irresponsible wits; glassy benighted men who are trying to remember they must see something of the exhibition to remember before they go home and try to describe it to their families;

young people, hand-in-love, who will giggle at whatever they see, at a goldfish in a pond, a model of the *Queen Elizabeth*, or a flint hammer; people too bored to yawn, long and rich as borzois, who, before they have seen it, have seen better shows in Copenhagen and San Francisco; eccentric people: men with their deerstalker caps tied with rope to their lapels, who carry dried nut sandwiches and little containers of yoghourt in hairy green knapsacks labelled 'glass with care'; fat, flustered women in as many layers of coats as an onion or a cab-driver, hunting in a fever through fifty fluffed pockets to find a lost packet of bird-seed they are going to give to the parrots who are not there; old scaly sneezing men, born of lizards in a snuff-bin, who read, wherever they go, from books in tiny print, and who never look up, even at the tureen-lid of the just-tethered dome or the shining skylon, the skygoing nylon, the cylindrical leg-of-the-future jetting, almost, to the exhibition of stars; *real* eccentrics: people who have come to the South Bank to study the growth and development of Britain from the Iron Age till now. Here they will find no braying pageantry, no taxidermal museum of Culture, no cold and echoing inhuman hygienic barracks of technical information, no shoddily cajoling emporium of tasteless Empire wares, but something very odd indeed, magical and parochial: a parish-pump made of flying glass and thistledown gauze-thin steel, a rolypoly pudding full of luminous, melodious bells, wheels, coils, engines and organs, alembics and jorums in a palace in thunderland sizzling with scientific witches' brews, a place of trains, bones, planes, ships, sheep, shapes, snipe, mobiles, marbles, brass bands, and cheese, a place painted regardless, and by hand.

Perhaps you'll think I'm shovelling the colour on too thickly; that I am, as it were, speaking under the influence of strong pink. (And what a lot of pink—rose, raspberry, strawberry, peach, flesh, blush, lobster, salmon, tally-ho—there is, plastered and doodled all over this four-acre gay and soon-to-be-gone Festival City in sprawling London.) London: to many of us who live in the country, the Capital punishment. Perhaps you will go on a cool, dull day, sane as a biscuit, and find that the exhibition does, indeed, tell the story 'of British contributions to world civilization in the arts of peace'; that, and nothing else. But I'm pleased to doubt it. Of *course* it is instructive; of *course* there is behind it an articulate and comprehensive plan; it can show you, unless you are an expert, more about, say, mineralogy or the ionosphere than you may want to know. It's bursting its buttons, in an orderly manner, with knowledge. But what everyone I know, and have observed, seems to like most in it is the gay, absurd, irrelevant, delighting imagination that flies and booms and spurts and trickles out of the whole bright boiling; the small stone oddity that squints at you round a sharp, daubed corner; the sexless abstract sculptures serenely and secretly existing out of time in old cold worlds of their own in places that appear, but only for one struck second, inappropriate; the linked terra-cotta man and woman fly-defying gravity and elegantly hurrying up a w.c. wall; the sudden design of hands on another wall, as though the painter had said: 'Oh, to the daft devil with what I'm doing,' and just slap-slap-slapped all over the ochre his spread-out fingers and thumbs, ten blunt arrows, or as though large convict-birds, if there are any such, had waddled up the wall and webbed it as they went. You see people go along briskly down the wide white avenues towards the pavilion of their fancy—'Our Humbert's dead keen on seeing the milk-separators'—and suddenly stop: another fancy swings or bubbles in front of their eyes. What is it they see? Indigo water waltzing to music. Row after row of rosy rolling balls spread on tall screens like the counting beads of Wellsian children fed on the food of the gods. Sheets of asbestos tied on to nowhere, by nothing, for nothing is anchored here and at the clap of hands the whole gallimaufry could take off to Sousa and zoom up the flagged sky. Small childbook-painted mobiles along the bridges that, at a flick of wind, become windmills and thrum round at night like rainbows with arms. Or the steel-and-platinum figure—created by the Welsh engineer and architect, Richard Huws—of maybe a mer-woman standing, if that is the word for one who grows out of it, in arc-light water; she weeps as she is wept on; first her glinting breast, then another plane of her, tips, slides, shoots, shelves, swings, and sidles out to take, from the lake of her birth, one ton of water at a time to Handel's *Water Music*, absorbs it, inhales it through dripping steel, then casts and cascades it off and out again. Or even the hundreds of little vivid steel chairs that look like hundreds of little vivid steel people sitting down.

In the pavilion called 'The Natural Scene,' see the seals and eagles, the foxes and wild cats, of these still wild islands, and the natural history of owled and cuckooed, ottered, unlikely London. A great naked tree climbs in the middle of all, with prodigious butterflies and beetles on it. A blackbird lights up, and the aviary's full of his singing; a thrush, a curlew, a skylark.

And, in the 'Country,' see all the sculpted and woven

loaves, in the shape of sheaves of wheat, in curls, plaits, and whirls. And men are thatching the roofs of cottages; and—what could be more natural?—the men are made of straw. And what a pleasure of baskets! Trugs, creels, pottles and punnets, heppers, dorsers and mounds, wiskets and whiskets. And if these are not the proper words, they should be.

In 'The Lion and the Unicorn' is celebrated, under flights of birds, the 'British Character,' that stubborn, stupid, seabound, lyrical, paradoxical dark farrago of uppishness, derring-do, and midsummer moonshine all fluting, snug, and copper-bottomed. Justice, for some reason, looms in the midst of the Hall, its two big wigs back to back, its black and scarlet robes falling below. The body of justice is shelves of law books. The black spaces beneath the white wigs looks like the profiles of eagles. The white knight rides there too, too much a Don Quixote for my looking-glass land, and very potless and panless. A bravo-ing hand pats his plaster back, and tells him good night. There is a machine for, I believe, grinding smoke. And a tea-set, I failed to see, of salmon bones. But, in all this authentically eccentric exhibition, it is the Eccentrics' Corner that is the most insipid. Some of the dullest exhibits in the pavilion are relieved by surrounding extravagance; but the department devoted to the rhapsodic inspirations of extravagance is by far the dullest. Why was not the exquisite talent utilized of the warlock who, offering his services to the Festival authorities, assured them he would, to order, throw a rainbow over the Thames? I wish he would throw a rainbow over me as I walk through the grey days. 'Yes, we can tell it's him coming,' the envious neighbours would murmur, 'we recognize his rainbow.' And, on the balcony, there is a row of tiny theatres; in each, the stage is set for a Shakespearian play; and out of the theatres come the words of the players. If you're in luck, something may go wrong with the works and Hamlet rant from Dunsinane.

In 'Homes and Gardens,' blink at the grievous furniture, ugly as sin and less comfy.

In the 'Transport Pavilions,' goggle at the wizard diesels and the smashing, unpuffing streamlines and the miracle model railway for dwarf nabobs.

Then, if there are by this time no spots in front of your eyes, go to the Telecinema and see them astonishingly all around you: spots with scarlet tadpole tails, and spottedly sinuous tintacks dancing with dissolving zebra heads, and blobs and nubbins and rubbery squirls receding, to zig-zag blasts of brass, down nasty polychrome corridors, a St Vitus's gala of abstract shapes and shades in a St Swithin's day of torrential dazzling darning needles. Sit still in the startling cinema and be kissed by a giraffe, who stretches his neck right out of the screen for you. Follow the deliberately coloured course of the Thames, the Royal River; the whispering water's more like water than water ever was; closer, closer, comes the slow king-fisher—blue water and suddenly it ripples all over you: that'll be the day when film stars do the same.

Go to the South Bank first by day; the rest of your times at night. Sit at a café table in the night of musical lights, by the radiant river, the glittering skylon above you rearing to be off, the lit pavilion, white, black, and silver in sweeps of stone and feathery steel, transplendent round you as you sip and think:

This is the first time I have ever truly seen that London whose sweet Thames runs softly; that minstrel mermaid of a town, the water-streeted eight-million-headed village in a blaze. *This* is London, not the huge petty misshaped nightmare I used to know as I hum-drummed along its graceless streets through fog and smoke and past the anonymous unhappy bodies lively as wet brollies. This Festival is London. The arches of the bridges leap into light; the moon clocks glow; the river sings; the harmonious pavilions are happy. And this is what London should always be like, till St Paul's falls down and the sea slides over the Strand.

The International Eisteddfod

Llangollen. A town in a vale in rolling green North Wales on a windy July morning. The sun squints out and is puffed back again into the grey clouds blowing, full to the ragged rims with rain, across the Berwyn Hills. The white-horsed River Dee hisses and paws over the hills of its stones and under the greybeard bridge. Wind smacks the river and you, it's a cold, cracking morning; birds hang and rasp over the whipped river, against their will, as though frozen still, or are wind-chaffed and scattered towards the gusty trees. As you drift down Castle Street with your hair flying, or your hat or umbrella dancing to be off and take the sky, you see and hear all about you the decorous, soberly dressed and headgeared, silent and unsmiling inhabitants of the tame town. You could be in any Welsh town on any windy snip of a morning, with only the birds and the river fuming and the only brightness the numberless greens and high purples of the hills. Everything is very ordinary in Llangollen; everything is nicely dull, except the summer world of wind and feathers, leaves and water. There is, if you are deaf, blind, and dumb, with a heart like cold bread pudding, nothing to remark or surprise. But rub your eyes with your black gloves. Here, over the bridge, come three Javanese, winged, breastplated, helmeted, carrying gongs and steel bubbles. Kilted, sporraned, tartan'd, daggered Scotsmen reel and strathspey up a side-street, piping hot. Burgundian girls, wearing, on their heads, bird-cages made of velvet, suddenly whisk on the pavement into a coloured dance. A viking goes into a pub. In black felt feathered hats and short leather trousers, enormous Austrians, with thighs big as Welshmen's bodies, but much browner, yodel to fiddles and split the rain with their smiles. Frilled, ribboned, sashed, fezzed, and white-turbaned, in baggy-blue sharavári and squashed red boots, Ukrainians with Manchester accents gopak up the hill. Everything is strange in Llangollen. You wish you had a scarlet hat, and bangles, and a little bagpipe to call your own, but it does not matter. The slapping bell-dancers, the shepherds and chamois-hunters, the fiddlers and fluters, the players on gongs and mandolines, guitars, harps, and trumpets, the beautiful flashing boys and girls of a score and more of singing countries, all the colours of the international rainbow, do not mind at all your mouse-brown moving among them: though you long, all the long Eisteddfod week, for a cloak like a blue sea or a bonfire to sweep and blaze in the wind, and a cap of bells, and a revelling waistcoat, and a great Alp-horn to blow all over Wales from the ruins of Dinas Brân.

Now follow your nose, and the noise of guitars, and the flying hues and flourish of those big singing-birds in their clogs and aprons and bonnets, veils, flowers, more flowers, and lace, past the wee Shoppes, through the babel of the bridge, by the very white policeman conducting from a rostrum, and up the tide of the hill, past popcorn and raspberryade, to the tented Field.

Green, packed banks run, swarming, down to the huge marquee there that groans and strains and sings in the sudden squalls like an airship crewed full of choirs. Music spills out of the microphones all over the humming field. Out of the wind-tugged tent it rises in one voice, and the crowd outside is hushed away into Spain. In a far corner of the field, young men and women begin to dance, for every reason in the world. Out skims the sun from a cloud-shoal. The spaniel ears of the little tents flap. Children collect the autographs of Dutch farmers. You hear a hive of summer hornets: it is the Burgundian *vielle*, a mandolin with a handle. Palestrina praises from Bologna to the choral picnickers. A Breton holiday sings in the wind, to clog-tramp and *biniou*.

Here they come, to this cup and echo of hills, people who love to make music, from France, Ireland, Norway, Italy, Switzerland, Spain, Java, and Wales: fine singers and faulty, nimble dancers and rusty, pipers to make the dead swirl or chanters with crows in their throats: all countries, shapes, ages, and colours, sword-dancers, court-dancers, cross-dancers, clog-dancers, dale-dancers, morris, ceilidhe, and highland, bolero, flamenco, heel-and-toe. They love to make music move. What a rush of dancing to Llangollen's feet! And, oh, the hubbub of tongues and toes in the dark chapels where every morning there's such a shining noise as you'd think would drive the Sunday bogles out of their doldrums for ever and ever.

Inside the vast marquee that drags at its anchors, eight thousand people—and you—face a sea of flowers, begonias, magnolias, lupins, lobelias, grown for these dancing days in the gardens of the town. Banks and waves of plants and flowers flow to the stage where a company from Holland—eight married pairs of them, the oldest in their late fifties, the youngest twenty or so—are performing, in sombre black, a country dance called, 'Throw Your Wife Away.' This is followed, appropriately and a little later, by a dance called, 'You Can't

Catch Me.' The movements of the humorous and simple dance are gay and sprightly. The men of the company dance like sad British railway-drivers in white clogs. Under their black, peaked caps, their faces are stern, weather-scored, and unrelenting. The quicker the music, the gloomier they clap and clog on the invisible cobbles of cold clean kitchens. The frenzied flute and fiddle whip them up into jet-black bliss as they frolic like undertakers. Long Dutch winter nights envelop them. Brueghel has painted them. They are sober as potatoes. Their lips move as they stamp and bow. Perhaps they are singing. Certainly, they are extremely happy.

And Austrians, then, to fiddles and guitar, sing a song of mowers in the Alpine meadows. Sworded Ukrainians—I mean, Ukrainians with swords—leap and kick above the planted sea. People from Tournas, in the Burgundy country, dance to accordion and *cabrette*, the Dance of the Vine—Dressers after Harvest. They plant the vines, put the leaves on the branches, hang up the grapes, pick the grapes, and press the wine. 'God gave us wine,' they sing as they dance, and the wine is poured into glasses and the dancers drink. (But the wine's not as real as the pussyfoot nudge and shudder down the aisles.)

All day the music goes on. Bell-padded, baldricked, and braided, those other foreigners, the English, dance fiercely out of the past, and some have beards, spade, gold, white, and black, to dance and wag as well.

And a chorus of Spanish ladies are sonorous and beautiful in their nighties.

And little girls from Obernkirchen sing like pigtailed angels.

All day the song and dancing in this transformed valley,

this green cup of countries in the country of Wales, goes on until the sun goes in. Then, in the ship of the tent, under the wind-filled sails, watchers and listeners grow slow and close into one cloud of shadow; they gaze, from their deep lulled dark, on to the lighted deck where the country dancers weave in shifting-coloured harvests of light.

And then you climb down hill again, in a tired tide, and over the floodlit Dee to the town that won't sleep for a whole melodious week or, if it does at all, will hear all night in its sleep the hills fiddle and strum and the streets painted with tunes.

The bars are open as though they could not shut and Sunday never come down over the fluting town like a fog or a shutter. For every reason in the world, there's a wave of dancing in the main, loud street. A fiddle at a corner tells you to dance and you do in the moon though you can't dance a step for all the Ukrainians in Llangollen. Peace plays on a concertina in the vigorous, starry street, and nobody is surprised.

When you leave the last voices and measures of the sweet-throated, waltzing streets, the lilt and ripple of the Dee leaping, and the light of the night, to lie down, and the strewn town lies down to sleep in its hills and ring of echoes, you will remember that nobody was surprised at the turn the town took and the life it danced for one week of the long, little year. The town sang and danced, as though it were right and proper as the rainbow or the rare sun to celebrate the old bright turning earth and its bullied people. Are you surprised that people still can dance and sing in a world on its head? The only surprising thing about miracles, however small, is that they sometimes happen.

A Visit to America

Across the United States of America, from New York to California and back, glazed, again, for many months of the year there streams and sings for its heady supper a dazed and prejudiced procession of European lecturers, scholars, sociologists, economists, writers, authorities on this and that and even, in theory, on the United States of America. And, breathlessly between addresses and receptions, in planes and trains and boiling hotel bedroom ovens, many of these attempt to keep journals and diaries. At first, confused and shocked by shameless profusion and almost shamed by generosity, unaccustomed to such importance as they are assumed, by their hosts, to possess, and up against the barrier of a common language, they write in their note-books like demons, generalizing away, on character and culture and the American political scene. But, towards the middle of their middle-aged whisk through middle-western clubs and universities, the fury of the writing flags; their spirits are lowered by the spirit with which they are everywhere strongly greeted and which, in ever-increasing doses, they themselves lower; and they begin to mistrust themselves, and their reputations—for they have found, too often, that an audience will receive a lantern-lecture on, say, ceramics, with the same uninhibited enthusiasm that it accorded the very week before to a paper on the Modern Turkish Novel. And, in their diaries, more and more do such entries appear as,

'No way of escape!' or 'Buffalo!' or 'I am beaten,' until at last they cannot write a word. And, twittering all over, old before their time, with eyes like rissoles in the sand, they are helped up the gangway of the home-bound liner by kind bosom friends (of all kinds and bosoms) who boister them on the back, pick them up again, thrust bottles, sonnets, cigars, addresses into their pockets, have a farewell party in their cabin, pick them up again, and, snickering and yelping, are gone: to wait at the dockside for another boat from Europe and another batch of fresh, green lecturers.

There they go, every spring, from New York to Los Angeles: exhibitionists, polemicists, histrionic publicists, theological rhetoricians, historical hoddy-doddies, balletomanes, ulterior decorators, windbags, and bigwigs and humbugs, men in love with stamps, men in love with steaks, men after millionaires' widows, men with elephantiasis of the reputation (huge trunks and teeny minds), authorities on gas, bishops, best sellers, editors looking for writers, writers looking for publishers, publishers looking for dollars, existentialists, serious physicists with nuclear missions, men from the B.B.C. who speak as though they had the Elgin Marbles in their mouths, potboiling philosophers, professional Irishmen (very lepri-corny), and I am afraid, fat poets with slim volumes. And see, too, in that linguaceous stream, the tall monocled men, smelling of saddle soap and club arm-chairs, their breath a nice blending of whisky and fox's blood, with big protruding upper-class tusks and county moustaches, presumably invented in England and sent abroad to advertise *Punch*, who lecture to women's clubs on such unlikely subjects as 'The History of Etching in the Shetland Islands.' And the brassy-bossy men-women, with corrugated-iron perms, and hippo hides, who come, self-announced, as 'ordinary British housewives,' to talk to rich minked chunks of American matronhood about the iniquity of the Health Services, the criminal sloth of the miners, the *visible* tail and horns of Mr Aneurin Bevan, and the fear of everyone in England to go out alone at night because of the organized legions of cosh boys against whom the police are powerless owing to the refusal of those in power to equip them with revolvers and to flog to ribbons every adolescent offender on any charge at all. And there shiver and teeter also, meek and driven, those British authors unfortunate enough to have written, after years of unadventurous forgotten work, one bad novel which became enormously popular on both sides of the Atlantic. At home, when success first hit them, they were mildly delighted; a couple of literary luncheons went sugar-tipsy to their heads, like the washing sherry served before those luncheons; and perhaps, as the lovely money rolled lushly in, they began to dream in their moony writers' way, of being able to retire to the country, keep wasps (or was it bees?), and never write another lousy word. But in come the literary agent's triggermen and the publisher's armed narks: 'You must go to the States and make a Personal Appearance. Your novel is *killing* them over there, and we're not surprised either. You must go round the States lecturing to women.' And the inoffensive writers, who've never dared lecture anyone, let alone women—they are frightened of women, they do not understand women, they write about women as creatures that never existed, and the women lap it up—these sensitive plants cry out: 'But what shall we lecture about?'

'The English Novel.'

'I don't read novels.'

'Great Women in Fiction.'

'I don't like fiction *or* women.'

But off they're wafted, first class, in the plush bowels of the *Queen Victoria* with a list of engagements long as a New York menu or a half-hour with a book by Charles Morgan, and soon they are losing their little cold-as-goldfish paw in the great general glutinous handshake of a clutch of enveloping hostesses. I think, by the way, that it was Ernest Raymond, the author of *Tell England*, who once made a journey round the American women's clubs, being housed and entertained at each small town he stopped at by the richest and largest and furriest lady available. On one occasion he stopped at some little station, and was met, as usual, by an enormous motor-car full of a large hornrimmed business man, looking *exactly* like a large hornrimmed business man on the films—and his roly-poly pearly wife. Mr Raymond sat with her in the back of the car, and off they went, the husband driving. At once, she began to say how utterly delighted she and her husband and the committee were to have him at their Women's Literary and Social Guild, and to compliment him on his books. 'I don't think I've ever, in all my life, enjoyed a book so much as *Sorrel and Son*,' she said. 'What you don't know about human nature! I think Sorrel is one of the most beautiful characters ever portrayed.'

Ernest Raymond let her talk on, while he stared, embarrassed, in front of him. All he could see were the three double chins that her husband wore at the back of his neck. On and on she gushed in praise of *Sorrel and Son* until he could stand it no longer. 'I quite agree with you,' he said. 'A beautiful book indeed. But I'm afraid I didn't write *Sorrel and Son*. It was written by an old friend of mine, Mr Warwick Deeping.'

And the large hornrimmed double-chinned husband at the wheel said without turning: 'Caught again, Emily.'

See the garrulous others, also, gabbing and garlanded from one nest of culture-vultures to another: people selling the English way of life and condemning the American way as they swig and guzzle through it; people resurrecting the theories of surrealism for the benefit of remote parochial female audiences who did not know it was dead, not having ever known it had been alive; people talking about Etruscan pots and pans to a bunch of dead pans and wealthy pots in Boston. And there, too, in the sticky thick of lecturers moving across the continent black with clubs, go the foreign poets, catarrhal troubadours, lyrical one-night-standers, dollar-mad nightingales, remittance-bards from at home, myself among them booming with the worst.

Did we pass one another, *en route*, all unknowing, I wonder, one of us, spry-eyed, with clean, white lectures and a soul he could call his own, going buoyantly west to his remunerative doom in the great State University factories, another returning dog-eared as his clutch of poems and his carefully typed impromptu asides? I ache for us both. There one goes, unsullied as yet, in his Pullman pride, toying, oh boy, with a blunderbuss bourbon, being smoked by a large cigar, riding out to the wide open spaces of the faces of his waiting audience. He carries, besides his literary baggage, a new, dynamic razor, just on the market, bought in New York, which operates at the flick of a thumb, but cuts the thumb to the bone; a tin of new shaving-lather which is worked with the other, unbleeding, thumb and covers not only the face but the whole bath-room and, instantly freezing, makes an arctic, icicled cave from which it takes two sneering bell-boys to extract him; and, of course, a nylon shirt. This, he dearly believed from the advertisements, he could himself wash in his hotel, hang to dry overnight, and put on, without ironing, in the morning. (In my case, no ironing *was* needed, for, as someone cruelly pointed out in print, I looked, anyway, like an unmade bed.)

He is vigorously welcomed at the station by an earnest crew-cut platoon of giant collegiates, all chasing the butterfly culture with net, note-book, poison-bottle, pin, and label, each with at least thirty-six terribly white teeth, and is nursed away, as heavily gently as though he were an imbecile rich aunt with a short prospect of life, into a motor-car in which, for a mere fifty miles or so travelled at poet-breaking speed, he assures them of the correctness of their assumption that he is half-witted by stammering inconsequential answers in an over-British accent to their genial questions about what international conference Stephen Spender might be attending at the moment or the reactions of British poets to the work of a famous American whose name he did not know or catch. He is then taken to a small party of only a few hundred people all of whom hold the belief that what a visiting lecturer needs before he trips on to the platform is just enough martinis so that he can trip *off* the platform as well. And, clutching his explosive glass, he is soon contemptuously dismissing, in a flush of ignorance and fluency, the poetry of those androgynous literary ladies with three names who produce a kind of verbal ectoplasm to order as a waiter dishes up spaghetti—only to find that the fiercest of these, a wealthy huntress of small, seedy lions (such as himself), who stalks the middle-western bush with ears and rifle cocked, is his hostess for the evening. Of the lecture he remembers little but the applause and maybe two questions: 'Is it true that the young English intellectuals are *really* psychological?' or, 'I always carry Kierkegaard in my pocket. What do you carry?'

Late at night, in his room, he fills a page of his journal with a confused, but scathing, account of his first engagement; summarizes American advanced education in a paragraph that will be meaningless to-morrow, and falls to sleep where he is immediately chased through long, dark thickets by a Mrs Mabel Frankincense Mehaffey, with a tray of martinis and lyrics.

And there goes the other happy poet bedraggedly back to New York which struck him all of a sheepish never-sleeping heap at first but which seems to him now, after the ulcerous rigours of a lecturer's spring, a haven cosy as toast, cool as an icebox, and safe as skyscrapers.

Laugharne

Off and on, up and down, high and dry, man and boy, I've been living now for fifteen years, or centuries, in this timeless, beautiful, barmy (both spellings) town, in this far, forgetful, important place of herons, cormorants (known here as billyduckers), castle, churchyard, gulls, ghosts, geese, feuds, scares, scandals, cherry-trees, mysteries, jackdaws in the chimneys, bats in the belfry, skeletons in the cupboards, pubs, mud, cockles, flatfish, curlews, rain, and human, often all too human, beings; and, though still very much a foreigner, I am hardly ever stoned in the streets any more, and can claim to be able to call several of the inhabitants, and a few of the herons, by their Christian names.

Now, some people live in Laugharne because they were born in Laugharne and saw no good reason to move; others migrated here, for a number of curious reasons, from places as distant and improbable as Tonypandy or even England, and have now been absorbed by the natives; some entered the town in the dark and immediately disappeared, and can sometimes be heard, on hushed black nights, making noises in ruined houses, or perhaps it is the white owls breathing close together, like ghosts in bed; others have almost certainly come here to escape the international police, or their wives; and there are those, too, who still do not know, and will never know, why they are here at all: you can see them, any day of the week, slowly, dopily, wandering up and down the streets like Welsh opium-eaters, half asleep in a heavy bewildered daze. And some, like myself, just came, one day, for the day, and never left; got off the bus, and forgot to get on again. Whatever the reason, if any, for our being here, in this timeless, mild, beguiling island of a town with its seven public-houses, one chapel in action, one church, one factory, two billiard tables, one St Bernard (without brandy), one policeman, three rivers, a visiting sea, one Rolls-Royce selling fish and chips, one cannon (cast-iron), one chancellor (flesh and blood), one port-reeve, one Danny Raye, and a multitude of mixed birds, here we just are, and there is nowhere like it anywhere at all.

But when you say, in a nearby village or town, that you come from this unique, this waylaying, old, lost Laugharne where some people start to retire before they start to work and where longish journeys, of a few hundred yards, are often undertaken only on bicycles, then, oh! the wary edging away, the whispers and whimpers, and nudges, the swift removal of portable objects!

'Let's get away while the going is good,' you hear.

'Laugharne's where they quarrel with boathooks.'

'All the women there's got web feet.'

'Mind out for the Evil Eye!'

'Never go there at the full moon!'

They are only envious. They envy Laugharne its minding of its own, strange, business; its sane disregard for haste; its generous acceptance of the follies of others, having so many, ripe and piping, of its own; its insular, featherbed air; its philosophy of 'It will all be the same in a hundred years' time.' They deplore its right to be, in their eyes, so wrong, and to enjoy it so much as well. And, through envy and indignation, they label and libel it a legendary lazy little black-magical bedlam by the sea. And is it? Of *course not*, I hope.

Return Journey

NARRATOR

It was a cold white day in High Street, and nothing to stop the wind slicing up from the docks, for where the squat and tall shops had shielded the town from the sea lay their blitzed flat graves marbled with snow and headstoned with fences. Dogs, delicate as cats on water, as though they had gloves on their paws, padded over the vanished buildings. Boys romped, calling high and clear, on top of a levelled chemist's and a shoe-shop, and a little girl, wearing a man's cap, threw a snowball in a chill deserted garden that had once been the Jug and Bottle of the Prince of Wales. The wind cut up the street with a soft sea-noise hanging on its arm, like a hooter in a muffler. I could see the swathed hill stepping up out of the town, which you never could see properly before, and the powdered fields of the roofs of Milton Terrace and Watkin Street and Fullers Row. Fish-frailed, netbagged, umbrella'd, pixie-capped, fur-shoed, blue-nosed, puce-lipped, blinkered like drayhorses, scarved, mittened, galoshed, wearing everything but the cat's blanket, crushes of shopping-women crunched in the little Lapland of the once grey drab street, blew and queued and yearned for hot tea, as I began my search through Swansea town cold and early on that wicked February morning. I went into the hotel. 'Good morning.'

The hall-porter did not answer. I was just another snowman to him. He did not know that I was looking for someone after fourteen years, and he did not care. He stood and shuddered, staring through the glass of the hotel door at the snowflakes sailing down the sky, like Siberian confetti. The bar was just opening, but already one customer puffed and shook at the counter with a full pint of half-frozen Tawe water in his wrapped-up hand. I said Good morning, and the barmaid, polishing the counter vigorously as though it were a rare and valuable piece of Swansea china, said to her first customer:

BARMAID

Seen the film at the Elysium Mr Griffiths there's snow isn't it did you come up on your bicycle our pipes burst Monday . . .

NARRATOR

A pint of bitter, please.

BARMAID

Proper little lake in the kitchen got to wear your Wellingtons when you boil a egg one and four please . . .

CUSTOMER

The cold gets me just here . . .

BARMAID

. . . and eightpence change that's your liver Mr Griffiths you been on the cocoa again . . .

NARRATOR

I wonder whether you remember a friend of mine?

He always used to come to this bar, some years ago. Every morning, about this time.

CUSTOMER

Just by here it gets me. I don't know what'd happen if I didn't wear a band . . .

BARMAID

What's his name?

NARRATOR

Young Thomas.

BARMAID

Lots of Thomases come here it's a kind of home from home for Thomases isn't it Mr Griffiths what's he look like?

NARRATOR

He'd be about seventeen or eighteen . . . (*Slowly*)

BARMAID

. . . I was seventeen once . . .

NARRATOR

. . . and above medium height. Above medium height for Wales, I mean, he's five foot six and a half. Thick blubber lips; snub nose; curly mousebrown hair; one front tooth broken after playing a game called Cats and Dogs, in the Mermaid, Mumbles; speaks rather fancy; truculent; plausible; a bit of a shower-off; plus-fours and no breakfast, you know; used to have poems printed in the *Herald of Wales*; there was one about an open-air performance of *Electra* in Mrs Bertie Perkins's garden in Sketty; lived up the Uplands; a bombastic adolescent provincial Bohemian with a thick-knotted artist's tie made out of his sister's scarf, she never knew where it had gone, and a cricket-shirt dyed bottle-green; a gabbing, ambitious, mock-tough, pretentious young man; and mole-y, too.

BARMAID

There's words what d'you want to find *him* for I wouldn't touch him with a barge-pole . . . would you, Mr Griffiths? Mind, you can never tell. I remember a man came here with a monkey. Called for 'alf for himself and a pint for the monkey. And he wasn't Italian at all. Spoke Welsh like a preacher.

NARRATOR

The bar was filling up. Snowy business bellies pressed their watch-chains against the counter; black business bowlers, damp and white now as Christmas puddings in their cloths, bobbed in front of the misty mirrors. The voice of commerce rang sternly through the lounge.

FIRST VOICE

Cold enough for you?

SECOND VOICE

How's your pipes, Mr Lewis?

THIRD VOICE

Another winter like this'll put paid to me, Mr Evans.

FOURTH VOICE

I got the 'flu . . .

FIRST VOICE

Make it a double . . .

SECOND VOICE

Similar . . .

BARMAID

Okay, baby . . .

CUSTOMER

I seem to remember a chap like you described. There couldn't be two like him let's hope. He used to work as a reporter. Down the Three Lamps I used to see him. Lifting his ikkle elbow. (*Confidentially*)

NARRATOR

What's the Three Lamps like now?

CUSTOMER

It isn't like anything. It isn't there. It's nothing mun. You remember Ben Evans's stores? It's right next door to that. Ben Evans isn't there either . . . (*Fade*)

NARRATOR

I went out of the hotel into the snow and walked down High Street, past the flat white wastes where all the shops had been. Eddershaw Furnishers, Curry's Bicycles,

Donegal Clothing Company, Doctor Scholl's, Burton Tailors, W. H. Smith, Boots Cash Chemists, Leslie's Stores, Upson's Shoes, Prince of Wales, Tucker's Fish, Stead & Simpson—all the shops bombed and vanished. Past the hole in space where Hodges & Clothiers had been, down Castle Street, past the remembered, invisible shops, Price's Fifty Shilling, and Crouch the Jeweller, Potter Gilmore Gowns, Evans Jeweller, Master's Outfitters, Style and Mantle, Lennard's Boots, True Form, Kardomah, R. E. Jones, Dean's Tailor, David Evans, Gregory Confectioners, Bovega, Burton's, Lloyd's Bank, and nothing. And into Temple Street. There the Three Lamps had stood, old Mac magisterial in his corner. And there the Young Thomas whom I was searching for used to stand at the counter on Friday paynights with Freddie Farr Half Hook, Bill Latham, Cliff Williams, Gareth Hughes, Eric Hughes, Glyn Lowry, a man among men, his hat at a rakish angle, in that snug, smug, select, Edwardian holy of best-bitter holies . . . (*Bar noises in background*)

OLD REPORTER

Remember when I took you down the mortuary for the first time, Young Thomas? He'd never seen a corpse before, boys, except old Ron on a Saturday night. 'If you want to be a proper newspaperman,' I said, 'you got to be well known in the right circles. You got to be *persona grata* in the mortuary, see.' He went pale green, mun.

FIRST YOUNG REPORTER

Look, he's blushing now . . .

OLD REPORTER

And when we got there what d'you think? The decorators were in at the mortuary, giving the old home a bit of a re-do like. Up on ladders having a slap at the roof. Young Thomas didn't see 'em, he had his pop eyes glued on the slab, and when one of the painters up the ladder said 'Good morning, gents' in a deep voice he upped in the air and out of the place like a ferret. Laugh!

BARMAID

(*Off*) You've had enough, Mr Roberts.
You heard what I said. (*Noise of a gentle scuffle*)

SECOND YOUNG REPORTER

(*Casually*) There goes Mr Roberts.

OLD REPORTER

Well fair do's they throw you out very genteel in this pub . . .

FIRST YOUNG REPORTER

Ever seen Young Thomas covering a soccer match down the Vetch and working it out in tries?

SECOND YOUNG REPORTER

And up the Mannesman Hall shouting 'Good footwork, sir,' and a couple of punch-drunk colliers galumphing about like jumbos.

FIRST YOUNG REPORTER

What you been reporting to-day, Young Thomas?

SECOND YOUNG REPORTER

Two typewriter Thomas the ace news-dick . . .

OLD REPORTER

Let's have a dekko at your note-book. 'Called at British Legion: Nothing. Called at Hospital: One broken leg. Auction at the Metropole. Ring Mr Beynon *re* Gymanfa Ganu. Lunch: Pint and pasty at the Singleton with Mrs Giles. Bazaar at Bethesda Chapel. Chimney on fire at Tontine Street. Walters Road Sunday School Outing. Rehearsal of the *Mikado* at Skewen'—all front page stuff . . . (*Fade*)

NARRATOR

The voices of fourteen years ago hung silent in the snow and ruin, and in the falling winter morning I walked on through the white havoc'd centre where once a very young man I knew had mucked about as chirpy as a sparrow after the sips and titbits and small change of the town. Near the *Evening Post* building and the fragment of the Castle I stopped a man whose face I thought I recognized from a long time ago. I said: I wonder if you can tell me . . .

PASSER-BY

Yes?

NARRATOR

He peered out of his blanketing scarves and from under his snowballed Balaclava like an Eskimo with a bad conscience. I said: If you can tell me whether you used to know a chap called Young Thomas. He worked on the *Post* and used to wear an overcoat sometimes with the check lining inside out so that you could play giant draughts on him. He wore a conscious woodbine, too . . .

PASSER-BY

What d'you mean, conscious woodbine?

NARRATOR

. . . and a perched pork pie with a peacock feather and he tried to slouch like a newshawk even when he was attending a meeting of the Gorseinon Buffalos . . .

PASSER-BY

Oh, *him*! He owes me half a crown. I haven't seen him since the old Kardomah days. He wasn't a reporter then, he'd just left the grammar school. Him and Charlie Fisher—Charlie's got whiskers now—and Tom Warner and Fred Janes, drinking coffee-dashes and arguing the toss.

NARRATOR

What about?

PASSER-BY

Music and poetry and painting and politics. Einstein and Epstein, Stravinsky and Greta Garbo, death and religion, Picasso and girls . . .

NARRATOR

And then?

PASSER-BY

Communism, symbolism, Bradman, Braque, the Watch Committee, free love, free beer, murder, Michelangelo, ping-pong, ambition, Sibelius, and girls . . .

NARRATOR

Is that all?

PASSER-BY

How Dan Jones was going to compose the most prodigious symphony, Fred Janes paint the most miraculously meticulous picture, Charlie Fisher catch the poshest trout, Vernon Watkins and Young Thomas write the most boiling poems, how they would ring the bells of London and paint it like a tart . . .

NARRATOR

And after that?

PASSER-BY

Oh the hissing of the butt-ends in the drains of the coffee-dashes and the tinkle and the gibble-gabble of the morning young lounge lizards as they talked about Augustus John, Emil Jannings, Carnera, Dracula, Amy Johnson, trial marriage, pocket-money, the Welsh sea, the London stars, King Kong, anarchy, darts, T. S. Eliot, and girls. . . . Duw, it's cold!

NARRATOR

And he hurried on, into the dervish snow, without a good morning or good-bye, swaddled in his winter woollens like a man in the island of his deafness, and I felt that perhaps he had never stopped at all to tell me of one more departed stage in the progress of the boy I was pursuing. The Kardomah Café was razed to the snow, the voices of the coffee-drinkers—poets, painters, and musicians in their beginnings—lost in the willynilly flying of the years and the flakes.

Down College Street I walked then, past the remembered invisible shops, Langley's, Castle Cigar Co., T. B. Brown, Pullar's, Aubrey Jeremiah, Goddard Jones, Richards, Hornes, Marles, Pleasance & Harper, Star Supply, Sidney Heath, Wesley Chapel, and nothing. . . . My search was leading me back, through pub and job and café, to the School. *(Fade)* *(School bell)*

SCHOOLMASTER

Oh yes, yes, I remember him well,
though I do not know if I would recognize him now:
nobody grows any younger, or better,
and boys grow into much the sort of men one would suppose
though sometimes the moustaches bewilder
and one finds it hard to reconcile one's memory of a small
none-too-clean urchin lying his way unsuccessfully out of his homework
with a fierce and many-medalled sergeant-major with three children or a divorced chartered accountant;
and it is hard to realize
that some little tousled rebellious youth whose only claim
to fame among his contemporaries was his undisputed right
to the championship of the spitting contest

is now perhaps one's own bank manager.
Oh yes, I remember him well, the boy you are searching for:
he looked like most boys, no better, brighter, or more respectful;
he cribbed, mitched, spilt ink, rattled his desk and
garbled his lessons with the worst of them;
he could smudge, hedge, smirk, wriggle, wince,
whimper, blarney, badger, blush, deceive, be
devious, stammer, improvise, assume
offended dignity or righteous indignation as though to the manner born;
sullenly and reluctantly he drilled, for some small
crime, under Sergeant Bird, so wittily nicknamed
Oiseau, on Wednesday half-holidays,
appeared regularly in detention classes,
hid in the cloakroom during algebra,
was, when a newcomer, thrown into the bushes of the
Lower Playground by bigger boys,
and threw newcomers into the bushes of the Lower
Playground when *he* was a bigger boy;
he scuffled at prayers,
he interpolated, smugly, the time-honoured wrong
irreverent words into the morning hymns,
he helped to damage the headmaster's rhubarb,
was thirty-third in trigonometry,
and, as might be expected, edited the School Magazine (*Fade*)

NARRATOR

The Hall is shattered, the echoing corridors charred where he scribbled and smudged and yawned in the long green days, waiting for the bell and the scamper into the Yard: the School on Mount Pleasant Hill has changed its face and its ways. Soon, they say, it may be no longer the School at all he knew and loved when he was a boy up to no good but the beat of his blood: the names are havoc'd from the Hall and the carved initials burned from the broken wood. But the names remain. What names did he know of the dead? Who of the honoured dead did he know such a long time ago? The names of the dead in the living heart and head remain for ever. Of all the dead whom did he know? (*Funeral bell*)

VOICE

Evans, K. J.
Haines, G. C.
Roberts, I. L.
Moxham, J.
Thomas, H.
Baines, W.
Bazzard, F. H.
Beer, L. J.
Bucknell, R.
Tywford, G.
Vagg, E. A.
Wright, G. (*Fade*)

NARRATOR

Then I tacked down the snowblind hill, a cat-o'-nine-gales whipping from the sea, and, white and eiderdowned in the smothering flurry, people padded past me up and down like prowling featherbeds. And I plodded through the ankle-high one cloud that foamed the town, into flat

Gower Street, its buildings melted, and along long Helen's Road. Now my search was leading me back to the seashore. *(Noise of sea, softly)*

NARRATOR

Only two living creatures stood on the promenade, near the cenotaph, facing the tossed crystal sea: a man in a chewed muffler and a ratting cap, and an angry dog of a mixed make. The man dithered in the cold, beat his bare blue hands together, waited for some sign from sea or snow; the dog shouted at the weather, and fixed his bloodshot eyes on Mumbles Head. But when the man and I talked together, the dog piped down and fixed his eyes on me, blaming me for the snow. The man spoke towards the sea. Year in, year out, whatever the weather, once in the daytime, once in the dark, he always came to look at the sea. He knew all the dogs and boys and old men who came to see the sea, who ran or gambolled on the sand or stooped at the edge of the waves as though over a wild, wide, rolling ash-can. He knew the lovers who went to lie in the sandhills, the striding masculine women who roared at their terriers like tiger tamers, the loafing men whose work it was in the world to observe the great employment of the sea. He said:

PROMENADE-MAN

Oh yes, yes, I remember him well, but I didn't know what was his name. I don't know the names of none of the sandboys. They don't know mine. About fourteen or fifteen years old, you said, with a little red cap. And he used to play by Vivian's Stream. He used to dawdle in the arches, you said, and lark about on the railway-lines and holler at the old sea. He'd mooch about the dunes and watch the tankers and the tugs and the banana boats come out of the docks. He was going to run away to sea, he said. *I* know. On Saturday afternoon he'd go down to the sea when it was a long way out, and hear the foghorns though he couldn't see the ships. And on Sunday nights, after chapel, he'd be swaggering with his pals along the prom, whistling after the girls. (*Titter*)

GIRL

Does your mother know you're out? Go away now. Stop following us. (*Another girl titters*)

GIRL

Don't you say nothing, Hetty, you're only encouraging. No thank *you*, Mr Cheeky, with your cut-glass accent and your father's trilby! I don't want *no* walk on *no* sands. What d'you say? Ooh listen to him, Het, he's swallowed a dictionary. No, I don't want to go with nobody up no lane in the moonlight, see, and I'm not a baby-snatcher neither. I seen you going to school along Terrace Road, Mr Glad-Eye, with your little satchel and wearing your red cap and all. You seen me wearing my . . . no you never. Hetty, mind your glasses! Hetty Harris, you're as bad as them. Oh go away and do your homework, you. No I'm not then. I'm nobody's homework, see. Cheek! Hetty Harris, don't you let him! Oooh, there's brazen! Well, just to the end of the prom, if you like. No further, mind . . .

PROMENADE-MAN

Oh yes, I knew him well. I've known him by the thousands . . .

NARRATOR

Even now, on the frozen foreshore, a high, far cry of boys, all like the boy I sought, slid on the glass of the streams and snowballed each other and the sky. Then I went on my way from the sea, up Brynmill Terrace and into Glanbrydan Avenue where Bert Trick had kept a grocer's shop and, in the kitchen, threatened the annihilation of the ruling classes over sandwiches and jelly and blancmange. And I came to the shops and houses of the Uplands. Here and around here it was that the journey had begun of the one I was pursuing through his past. (*Old piano cinema-music in background*)

FIRST VOICE

Here was once the flea-pit picture-house where he whooped for the scalping Indians with Jack Basset and banged for the rustlers' guns.

NARRATOR

Jackie Basset, killed.

THIRD VOICE

Here once was Mrs Ferguson's, who sold the best gob-stoppers and penny packets full of surprises and a sweet kind of glue.

FIRST VOICE

In the fields behind Cwmdonkin Drive, the Murrays chased him and all cats.

SECOND VOICE

No fires now where the outlaws' fires burned and the paradisiacal potatoes roasted in the embers.

THIRD VOICE

In the Graig beneath Town Hill he was a lonely killer hunting the wolves (or rabbits) and the red Sioux tribe (or Mitchell brothers).

(Fade cinema-music into background of children's voices reciting, in unison, the names of the counties of Wales)

FIRST VOICE

In Mirador School he learned to read and count. Who made the worst raffia doilies? Who put water in Joyce's galoshes, every morning prompt as prompt? In the afternoons, when the children were good, they read aloud from Struwelpeter. And when they were bad, they sat alone in the empty classroom, hearing, from above them, the distant, terrible, sad music of the late piano lesson.

(The children's voices fade. The piano lesson continues in background)

NARRATOR

And I went up, through the white Grove, into Cwmdonkin Park, the snow still sailing and the childish, lonely, remembered music fingering on in the suddenly gentle wind. Dusk was folding the Park around, like another, darker snow. Soon the bell would ring for the closing of the gates, though the Park was empty. The park-keeper walked by the reservoir, where swans had glided, on his white rounds. I walked by his side and asked him my questions, up the swathed drives past buried beds and loaded utterly still furred and birdless trees towards the last gate. He said:

PARK-KEEPER

Oh yes, yes, I knew him well. He used to climb the reservoir railings and pelt the old swans. Run like a billygoat over the grass you should keep off of. Cut branches off the trees. Carve words on the benches. Pull up moss in the rockery, go snip through the dahlias. Fight in the bandstand. Climb the elms and moon up the top like a owl. Light fires in the bushes. Play on the green bank. Oh yes, I knew him well. I think he was happy all the time. I've known him by the thousands.

NARRATOR

We had reached the last gate. Dusk drew around us and the town. I said: What has become of him now?

PARK-KEEPER

Dead.

NARRATOR

The Park-keeper said:

(The park bell rings)

PARK-KEEPER

Dead . . . Dead . . . Dead . . . Dead . . . Dead . . . Dead.

PART II

Wilfred Owen

This book is not about heroes. English Poetry is not yet fit to speak of them. Nor is it about deeds or lands, nor anything about glory, honour, dominion or power,
except War.
Above all, this book is not concerned with Poetry.
The subject of it is War, and the pity of War.
The Poetry is in the pity.
Yet these elegies are not to this generation,
This is in no sense consolatory.

They may be to the next.
All the poet can do to-day is to warn.
That is why the true Poets must be truthful.

And that is the preface, by Wilfred Owen, to a volume of his poems which was to show, to England, and the intolerant world, the foolishness, unnaturalness, horror, inhumanity, and insupportability of war, and to expose, so that all could suffer and see, the heroic lies, the willingness of the old to sacrifice the young, indifference, grief, the soul of soldiers.

The volume, as Wilfred Owen visualized it in trench and shellhole and hospital, in the lunatic centre of battle, in the collapsed and apprehensive calm of sick-leave, never appeared. But many of the poems that were to have been included in the volume remain, their anguish unabated, their beauty for ever, their truth manifest, their warning unheeded.

Wilfred Owen was born in 1893 and killed in 1918. Twenty-five years of age, he was the greatest poet of the First Great War. Perhaps, in the future, if there are men, then, still to read—by which I mean, if there are men at all—he may be regarded as one of the great poets of all wars. But only war itself can resolve the problem of the ultimate truth of his, or of anyone else's poetry: war, or its cessation.

And this time, when, in the words of an American critic, the audiences of the earth, witnessing what well may be the last act of their own tragedy, insist upon chief actors who are senseless enough to perform a cataclysm, the voice of the poetry of Wilfred Owen speaks to us, down the revolving stages of thirty years, with terrible new significance and strength. We had not forgotten his poetry, but perhaps we had allowed ourselves to think of it as the voice of one particular time, one place, one war. Now, at the beginning of what, in the future, may never be known to historians as the 'atomic age'—for obvious reasons: there may be no historians—we can see, re-reading Owen, that he is a poet of all times, all places, and all wars. There is only one war: that of men against men.

Owen left to us less than sixty poems, many of them complete works of art, some of them fragments, some of them in several versions of revision, the last poem of them all dying away in the middle of a line. . . . 'Let us sleep now. . . .' I shall not try to follow his short life, from the first imitations of his beloved Keats to the last prodigious whisper of 'sleep' down the profound and echoing tunnels of 'Strange Meeting.' Mr Edmund Blunden, in the introduction to his probably definitive edition of the poems, has done that with skill and love. His collected poems make a little, huge book, working —and always he worked on his poems like fury, or a poet—from a lush ornamentation of language, brilliantly, borrowed melody, and ingenuous sentiment, to dark, grave, assonant rhythms, vocabulary purged and sinewed, wrathful pity and prophetic utterance.

But these are all words, my words. Let us hear him, before we try to see him, in some kind of flame-lit perspective, on the battlefields of France and the Earth. This poem is called 'Exposure.'

I

Our brains ache, in the merciless iced east winds that
knife us . . .
Wearied we keep awake because the night is silent . . .
Low drooping flares confuse our memory of the
salient . . .
Worried by silence, sentries whisper, curious, nervous,
But nothing happens.

Watching, we hear the mad gusts tugging on the wire.
Like twitching agonies of men among its brambles.
Northward incessantly, the flickering gunnery rumbles,
Far off, like a dull rumour of some other war.
What are we doing here?

The poignant misery of dawn begins to grow . . .
We only know war lasts, rain soaks, and clouds sag stormy.
Dawn massing in the east her melancholy army
Attacks once more in ranks on shivering ranks of gray,
But nothing happens.

Sudden successive flights of bullets streak the silence.
Less deadly than the air that shudders black with snow,
With sidelong flowing flakes that flock, pause and renew,
We watch them wandering up and down the wind's nonchalance,
But nothing happens.

II

Pale flakes with lingering stealth come feeling for our faces—
We cringe in holes, back on forgotten dreams, and stare, snow-dazed,
Deep into grassier ditches. So we drowse, sun-dozed,
Littered with blossoms trickling where the blackbird fusses.
Is it that we are dying?

Slowly our ghosts drag home: glimpsing the sunk fires glozed
With crusted dark-red jewels; crickets jingle there;
For hours the innocent mice rejoice: the house is theirs;
Shutters and doors all closed: on us the doors are closed—
We turn back to our dying.

Since we believe not otherwise can kind fires burn;
Now ever suns smile true on child, or field, or fruit.
For God's invincible spring our love is made afraid;
Therefore, not loath, we lie out here; therefore were born,
For love of God seems dying.

To-night, His frost will fasten on this mud and us,
Shrivelling many hands and puckering foreheads crisp.
The burying-party, picks and shovels in their shaking grasp,
Pause over half-known faces. All their eyes are ice,
But nothing happens.

Who wrote this? A boy of twenty-three or four, comfortably born and educated, serious, 'literary,' shy, never 'exposed' before to anything harsher than a Channel-crossing, fond of *Endymion* and the open air, fresh from a tutor's job. Earlier, in letters to his mother, he had written from the Somme, in 1917, in that infernal winter: 'There is a fine heroic feeling about being in France, and I am in perfect spirits.' . . . Or again, he talked of his companions: 'The roughest set of knaves I have ever been herded with.' When he heard the guns for the first time, he said: 'It was a sound not without a certain sublimity.'

It was *this* young man, at first reacting so conventionally to his preconceived ideas of the 'glory of battle' and such ideas—he was to slash and scorify a very short time afterwards—who wrote the poem. It was this young man, steel-helmeted, buff-jerkined, gauntleted, rubber-wadered, in the freezing rain of the flooded trenches, in the mud that was not mud, but an octopus of sucking clay, who wrote 'Anthem for Doomed Youth.'

What passing-bells for these who die as cattle?
    Only the monstrous anger of the guns.
    Only the stuttering rifles' rapid rattle
Can patter out their hasty orisons.

No mockeries for them; no prayers nor bells,
Nor any voice of mourning save the choirs,—
The shrill, demented choirs of wailing shells;
And bugles calling for them from sad shires.

What candles may be held to speed them all?
    Not in the hands of boys, but in their eyes
Shall shine the holy glimmers of goodbyes.
    The pallor of girls' brows shall be their pall;
Their flowers the tenderness of patient minds,
And each slow dusk a drawing-down of blinds.

There is no contradiction here. The studious, healthy young man with a love of poetry, as we see him set against the safe background of school, university, and tutordom, is precisely the same as the sombre but radiant, selfless, decrying and exalting, infinitely tender, humble, harrowed seer and stater of the anthem for Doomed Youth and for himself. There is no difference. Only, the world has happened to him. And everything, as Yeats once said, happens in a blaze of light.

The world had happened to him. All its suffering moved about and within him. And his intense pity for all human fear, pain, and grief was given trumpet-tongue. He knew, as surely as though the words had been spoken to him aloud, as indeed they had been though they were the words of wounds, the shape of the dead, the colour of blood, he knew he stood alone among men to *plead* for them in their agony, to blast the walls of ignorance, pride, pulpit, and state. He stood like Everyman, in no man's land:

> It is like the eternal place of gnashing of teeth; the Slough of Despond could not be contained in one of its crater-holes; the fires of Sodom and Gomorrah could not light a candle to it—to find a way to *Babylon the Fallen*.

And out of this, he wrote the poem called 'Greater Love.'

Red lips are not so red
  As the stained stones kissed by the English dead.
Kindness of wooed and wooer
Seems shame to their love pure.
O Love, your eyes lose lure
    When I behold eyes blinded in my stead!

Your slender attitude
    Trembles not exquisite like limbs knife-skewed,
Rolling and rolling there
Where God seems not to care;
Till the fierce Love they bear
    Cramps them in death's extreme decrepitude.

Your voice sings not so soft,—
Though even as wind murmuring through raftered loft,—
Your dear voice is not dear,
Gentle, and evening clear,
As theirs whom none now hear
Now earth has stopped their piteous mouths that coughed.

Heart, you were never hot,
Nor large, nor full like hearts made great with shot;
And though your hand be pale,
Paler are all which trail
Your cross through flame and hail:
Weep, you may weep, for you may touch them not.

It was impossible for him to avoid the sharing of suffering. He could not record a wound that was not his own. He had so very many deaths to die, and so very short a life within which to endure them all. It's no use trying to imagine what would have happened to Owen had he lived on. Owen, at twenty-six or so, exposed to the hysteria and exploded values of false peace. Owen alive now, at the age of fifty-three, and half the world starving. You cannot generalize about age and poetry. A man's poems, if they are good poems, are always older than himself; and sometimes they are ageless. We know that the shape and the texture of his poems would always be restlessly changing, though the purpose behind them would surely remain unalterable; he would always be experimenting technically, deeper and deeper driving towards the final intensity of language: the words behind words. Poetry is, of its nature, an experiment. All poetical impulses are towards the creation of adventure. And adventure is movement. And the end of each adventure is a new impulse to move again towards creation. Owen, had he lived, would never have ceased experiment; and so powerful was the impetus behind his work, and so intricately strange his always growing mastery of words, he would never have ceased to influence the work of his contemporaries. Had he lived, English poetry would not be the same. The course of poetry is dictated by accidents. Even so, he is one of the four most profound influences upon the poets who came after him; the other three being Gerard Manley Hopkins, the later W. B. Yeats, and T. S. Eliot.

But we must go back, from our guesses and generalizations and abstractions, to Owen's poetry itself; to the brief, brave life and the enduring words. In hospital, labelled as a 'neurasthenic case,' he observed, and experienced, the torments of the living dead, and he has expressed their 'philosophy' in the dreadful poem, 'A Terre.'

(Being the philosophy of many Soldiers)

Sit on the bed; I'm blind, and three parts shell,
Be careful; can't shake hands now; never shall.
Both arms have mutinied against me—brutes.
My fingers fidget like ten idle brats.
I tried to peg out soldierly—no use!
One dies of war like any old disease.
This bandage feels like pennies on my eyes.

I have my medals?—Discs to make eyes close.
My glorious ribbons?—Ripped from my own back
In scarlet shreds. (That's for your poetry book.)

A short life and a merry one, my brick!
We used to say we'd hate to live dead old,—
Yet now . . . I'd willingly be puffy, bald,
And patriotic. Buffers catch from boys
At least the jokes hurled at them. I suppose
Little I'd ever teach a son, but hitting,
Shooting, war, hunting, all the arts of hurting.
Well, that's what I learnt,—that, and making money.
Your fifty years ahead seem none too many?
Tell me how long I've got? God! For one year
To help myself to nothing more than air!
One Spring! Is one too good to spare, too long!
Spring wind would work its own way to my lung,
And grow me legs as quick as lilac-shoots.
My servant's lamed, but listen how he shouts!
When I'm lugged out, he'll still be good for that.
Here in this mummy-case, you know, I've thought
How well I might have swept his floors for ever,
I'd ask no night off when the bustle's over,
Enjoying so the dirt. Who's prejudiced
Against a grimed hand when his own's quite dust,
Less live than specks that in the sun-shafts turn,
Less warm than dust that mixes with arms' tan?
I'd love to be a sweep, now, black as Town,
Yes, or a muckman. Must I be his load?
O Life, Life, let me breathe,—a dug-out rat!
Not worse than ours the existences rats lead–
Nosing along at night down some safe vat,

They find a shell-proof home before they rot.
Dead men may envy living mites in cheese,
Or good germs even. Microbes have their joys,
And subdivide, and never come to death,
Certainly flowers have the easiest time on earth.
'I shall be one with nature, herb, and stone.'
Shelley would tell me. Shelley would be stunned;
The dullest Tommy hugs that fancy now.
'Pushing up daisies,' is their creed, you know.
To grain, then, go my fat, to buds my sap,
For all the usefulness there is in soap.
D'you think the Boche will ever stew man-soup?
Some day, no doubt, if . . .
Friend, be very sure
I shall be better off with plants that share
More peaceably the meadow and the shower.
Soft rains will touch me,—as they could touch once,
And nothing but the sun shall make me ware.
Your guns may crash around me. I'll not hear;
Or, if I wince, I shall not know I wince.
Don't take my soul's poor comfort for your jest.
Soldiers may grow a soul when turned to fronds,
But here the thing's best left at home with friends.

My soul's a little grief, grappling your chest,
To climb your throat on sobs; easily chased
On other sighs and wiped by fresher winds.

Carry my crying spirit till it's weaned
To do without what blood remained these wounds.

To see him in his flame-lit perspective, against the background, now of the poxed and cratered war-scape, shivering in the snow under the slitting wind, marooned on a frozen desert, or crying, in a little oven of mud, that his 'senses are charred,' is to see a man consigned to articulate immolation. He buries his smashed head with his own singed hands, and is himself the intoning priest over the ceremony, the suicide, the sunset. He is the common touch. He is the bell of the church of the broken body. He writes love-letters home for the illiterate dead. Ignorant, uncaring, hapless as the rest of the bloody troops, he is their arguer shell-shocked into diction, though none may understand. He is content to be the unhonoured prophet in death's country: for fame, as he said, was the last infirmity he desired.

None of the poems you have heard were published while Owen was alive; indeed, he saw little or nothing of his in print. But I don't want to give the impression that he wrote always in intellectual loneliness, or that he carried his poems about with him like dark, incommunicable secrets. Siegfried Sassoon has described how, when he was in a nursing-home for what were then called 'shell-shock cases,' Owen, a stranger, came into his room with a number of Sassoon's newly published book of poems, and, shyly, asked him if he would autograph them. And Sassoon and Owen talked about poetry; Sassoon, as he himself said, rather laying down the law to this unassuming, shy young man. And Owen, on leaving, gave him some poems and asked him if he'd have a look at them and tell him if they were any good. And Sassoon saw that they were good. And so did several other poets and men of letters to whom Sassoon sent them. And arrangements were made for a book of them to be published. Owen never saw that book.

There are many aspects of Owen's life and work upon which I haven't touched at all. I have laboured, in these notes or pieces between poems, only one argument, and that inherent in the poems themselves. Owen's words have shown, for me, and I hope (and know) for you, the position-in-calamity which, without intellectual choice, he chose to take. But remember, he was not a 'wise man' in the sense that he had achieved, for himself, a true way of believing. He believed there was no one true way because all ways are by-tracked and rutted and pitfalled with ignorance and injustice and indifference. He was himself diffident and self-distrustful. He had to be wrong; clumsy; affected often; ambiguous; bewildered. Like every man at last, he had to fight the whole war by himself. He lost, and he won. In a letter written towards the end of his life and many deaths, he quoted from Rabindranath Tagore: 'When I go hence, let this be my parting word, that what I have seen is unsurpassable.'

He was killed on 4th November 1918. This is his last, and unfinished poem, found among his papers after his death, 'Strange Meeting.'

It seemed that out of the battle I escaped
Down some profound dull tunnel, long since scooped
Through granites which Titanic wars had groined.
Yet also there encumbered sleepers groaned,
Too fast in thought or death to be bestirred.
Then, as I probed them, one sprang up, and stared
With piteous recognition in fixed eyes,

Lifting distressful hands as if to bless.
And by his smile, I knew that sullen hall;
With a thousand fears that vision's face was grained;
Yet no blood reached there from the upper ground,
And no guns thumped, or down the flues made moan.
'Strange, friend,' I said, 'Here is no cause to mourn.'
'None,' said the other, 'Save the undone years,
The hopelessness. Whatever hope is yours,
Was my life also; I went hunting wild
After the wildest beauty in the world,
Which lies not calm in eyes, or braided hair,
But mocks the steady running of the hour,
And if it grieves, grieves richlier than here.
For by my glee might many men have laughed,
And of my weeping something has been left,
Which must die now. I mean the truth untold,
The pity of war, the pity war distilled.
Now men will go content with what we spoiled.
Or, discontent, boil bloody, and be spilled.
They will be swift with swiftness of the tigress,
None will break ranks, though nations trek from
progress.
Courage was mine, and I had mystery;
Wisdom was mine, and I had mastery;
To miss the march of this retreating world
Into vain citadels that are not walled.
Then, when much blood had clogged their chariot-
wheels
I would go up and wash them from sweet wells,
Even with truths that lie too deep for taint.
I would have poured my spirit without stint
But not through wounds; not on the cess of war.
Foreheads of men have bled where no wounds were.

I am the enemy you killed, my friend.
I knew you in this dark; for so you frowned
Yesterday through me as you jabbed and killed.
I parried; but my hands were loath and cold.
Let us sleep now . . .'

Walter de la Mare as a Prose Writer

> 'What I say is, keep on this side of the tomb as long as you can. Don't meddle with that hole. Why? Because while some fine day you will have to go down into it, you can never be quite sure while you are here what mayn't come back out of it.
>
> '*There'll be no partings there*—I have heard them trolling that out in their chapels like missel-thrushes in the spring. They seem to forget there may be some mighty unpleasant *meetings.* And what about the further shore? It's my belief there's some kind of a ferry plying on that river. And coming back depends on what you want to come back *for.*'

So an old, smallish man, muffled in a very respectable greatcoat at least two sizes too large for him, mutters in a dark corner of the firelit station waiting-room in Walter de la Mare's uneasy story, *Crewe.*

How many of the nasty ghosts, from the other side of the razor's edge, from the wrong room, from the chockablock grave, from the trespassing hereafter, from the sly holes, crawl over and into the seedy waiting-rooms, the creeping railway carriages, the gas-lamped late-Victorian teashops the colour of stewed tea, where down-at-soul strangers contrive their tales and, drop by drop, leak out the shadows of their grey or black, forlorn, and vaguely infernal secrets. The ghosts of Mr de la Mare, though they reek and scamper, and, in old houses at the proper bad hours, are heard sometimes at their infectious business, are not for you to see. But there is no assurance that they do not see you.

And remember, in Mr de la Mare, the scarecrow that suddenly appears in a cornfield behind a house where lately a man has hanged himself. '"Does the air round the scarecrow strike you as funny at all?" I asked him. "Out of the way funny—quivering, in a manner of speaking?" "That's the heat," he said, but his lip trembled.' And the shocking, hallucinatory mask of face and head lying on Mr Bloom's pillow. And the polluted, invisible presences that seep through the charnel-house of Seaton's bloated and grave-emptying Aunt. Here in this house, and in all the other drenched, death-storied houses, down whose corridors and staircases the past hisses, and in whose great mirrors you see behind you a corridor of hinted faces, and in whose lofty beds you share your sheets and nightmare with an intangible, shifted fellow or the sibilant echo of a sound you wish had never been made, most things that happen are ordinary, or very nearly ordinary, and vile. These are houses suspended in time; and timelessness erupts in them.

Mr de la Mare's *first* world of childhood is as 'phantasmal' and 'solitary' as Hans Andersen's, but rarely so cruel—or so alive. We grow to know that a huge mythological distance separates that world where Kay and Gerda breathe for ever and that in which the child-alone of de la Mare's tall tales go about their dreams, loves, and surprises. The country whose habitations, whose great sleepy meadows of March mornings, blue and tumultous and bleak, far away cold towers and pinnacles, whether of clouds or hills, valleys and spelled woods, grey-green dells, mistletoed and mustard-seeded avenues, that the children of his earliest stories people, infest, and, to high music, moon, glide, and meander through, this is a country of books. Hans Andersen's characters move in a magic that was not, beforehand, composed, pictured, or written down, but is created, there and then, by their lovely motion, and for themselves alone to inhabit. But in, for example, *Henry Brocken*, the first of de la Mare's long tales, the world through which the beguiled boy wanders on his mild Rosinante is made of the trees and climates, moors, mornings and evenings, groves, hills, suns, stars, and gardens, of written, remembered words, of Bunyan's allegory and Swift's satire, of the poetry of Wordsworth, Herrick, Shakespeare, Poe, and Keats. Here enamoured Henry Brocken, in the library country, roving deep in the coils of the necromantic ball, meets Lucy Gray, Jane Eyre, Julia, Electra, Dianeme, Anthea, Nick Bottom, the Sleeping Beauty, Gulliver, La Belle Dame Sans Merci, Annabel Lee. But, overdecorated, remote, rooted in 'reverie,' that favourite woollen-headed word, the adventure is all shades. *Henry Brocken* is a bookish and starry-eyed mood on a borrowed horse. The fabled earth is cloud. Clouds are reflections and echoes of sea-waves that rhyme with other words. Rarely just pretty or arch, the way of the story is too often sadly sweet and single-noted.

But as Mr de la Mare went on writing, his children went on growing. They did not grow into youths but into children. They lost that lorn and dewy wonder, and when they moved, though always on odd errands, they did not rustle like the pages of an old book turned in a lamplit brown study by a wan, near-tenuous, but inky hand. 'Homesick,' 'forlorn,' 'lost,' and 'silent'—these words were used less often, though the nostalgia for the 'mournful gaiety' of the past, the loneliness, the silence, and the delirium, still were there.

It was through Mr de la Mare's perception of the very natural oddity and immediacy of childhood that a story like *The Almond Tree* emerged, most movingly, out of the tapestried and *unnatural* 'farness' of *Henry Brocken*.

Nicholas in *The Almond Tree* is, in Mr Forrest Reid's words, 'the first of a line of strange, wayward, intelligent, dangerously sensitive, infinitely alive small boys.' In later stories his name changes, he is older or younger, sadder or gayer, more darkly cunning or more coldly innocent, now embroiled and tangled in briery thickets of love, now critical and aloof, faintly smiling, in fear and evil occurrences; but always his eyes are the same. It is through these eyes we see the astonishing systems, the unpredictable order, of life on the edge of its answer or quivering on a poisonous threshold.

Only on slight occasions do Mr de la Mare's children come into contact with each other. We see them, nearly always, in their relation to abnormal men and women. And, of his children, it is only the small boys who become real. The little girls live in a distant, and more fragile, past.

A '*more* fragile' past; for he is loyal, always, to old Ways and Days, old houses, regions, customs, scents, and colours. His children loiter, wonder, and perceive, his men and women suffer, love, and are haunted, his weathers happen, his dead-behind-the-wainscot blow and scamper, in a time and place that was before he was born. The life of his countryside is that which his mother remembered hearing *her* mother tell of, and of which she told him when he was a child. His imagined memories of childhood are all of a timeless past before his own.

Mr de la Mare's stories first appeared about 1900. One of the first reviewers to recognize his awakening genius was Francis Thompson. Through all those intermediary years he has written long and short stories, for children, about children, for grown men and dead men, for the unborn, for a livelihood, for nothing, for the best reward, through innocence and with wide and deep skill, for pleasure, for fun, from suffering, and for himself.

His influences? Sir Thomas Browne, de Quincey, Ecclesiastes, Henry James, Emily Brontë, Stevenson, Poe, Traherne. And, in later life, Julian Greene perhaps? His style? It is his stories. At the very beginning he was fond, I think, of a rather flowery verbosity; he used a lot of clichés, but they were always the right ones. There was the suggestion of something, even in a young man, old-maidenish about his attitude to the love of men for women. Country terror was a little cosy, so that you felt not that something nasty had happened in the woodshed but that there were quite hellish goings-on among the wool-baskets in the parlour. The period and place about which he writes? Somewhere in rural England, say anywhere after 1830 and just before the after-life. In his more mature dramatic stories about grown-up human relationships, he often used a convoluted monologue-manner that occasionally suggested the ghost of a landbound Conrad talking from behind a pot of ferns. A fault of the prose style, always avoided in the verse, was a gravy-like thickening of texture. And his elaborate language, fuller than ever of artifice and allusion when it was seemingly simple, did not suit, to my mind, the more-or-less straightforward, or the grotesque fairy-story. His *real* fairies are as endearing as Dracula. And his subject, always, is the imminence of spiritual danger.

Sir Philip Sidney

It is among the arguments of the *Defence of Poesie* that the poet is the greatest teacher of knowledge because he teaches by a divine delightfulness.

'For,' wrote Sir Philip Sidney,

> he doth not only show the way, but giveth so sweet a prospect into the way as will entice any man to enter into it. Nay, he doth, as if your journey should lie through a fair vineyard, at the very first, give you a cluster of grapes, that full of that taste, you may long to pass further. He beginneth not with obscure definitions, which must blur the margent with interpretations, and load the memory with doubtfulness, but he cometh to you with words set in delightful proportion, either accompanied with, or prepared for the well enchanting skill of music; and with a tale forsooth he cometh unto you, with a tale, which holdeth children from play, and old men from the chimney corner.

The Defence of Poesie is a defence of the imaginative life, of the duty, and the delight, of the individual poet living among men in the middle of the turning world that has, in his time, so little time for him. Sometimes melancholy, often distant, proud and politic, delicate and hot-headed, unperturbedly honest, he exercised a grave fascination upon all who met him. He deliberated upon himself with gravity, and found it delightful or distasteful as the wind of love blew, as the life of Elizabeth's court grew perilous, lax, fickle, or degraded, as shallow justice shook, as adventurers sailed with wrong maps round the real rich roaring globe.

Even when he was a child at Penshurst or in Wales, his parents, seeing him such a grave boy, 'adjured him to be merry.' He was praised, while a child, by Fulke Greville, for being of 'such staidness of mind, lovely and familiar gravity, as carried grace and reverence above greater years.'

Sir Philip Sidney's mother was the daughter of John Dudley, the Duke of Northumberland who was beheaded for his part in the placing of Lady Jane Grey upon the throne of England. That little reign brought death and desolation to all his mother's kin. Sidney could never have forgotten what his mother must have told him: Lady Mary Sidney who nursed Queen Elizabeth through smallpox and who caught the disease herself so horribly that, even at home, she always wore a mask: he never could have forgotten that Guildford Dudley, his mother's brother, married Jane Grey; that on her way to be made queen, dressed in green velvet, she was so slight and small she was mounted on very high chopines to make her look taller. 'She was sixteen, Guildford was a very tall strong boy with light hair, who paid her much attention.' On her way to the scaffold she carried a prayer book, and wore black.

Sidney's father, Sir Henry, was the ablest governor of Ireland under Elizabeth. He wrote to his very young son, then a scholar at Shrewsbury School, this mature advice:

> Seldom drink wine, and yet sometimes do, lest being enforced to drink upon the sudden you should find yourself inflamed.

Be courteous of gesture and affable to all men, with diversity of reverences according to the dignity of the person: there is nothing that winneth so much for so little cost.

Give yourself to be merry, for you degenerate from your father if you find not yourself most able in wit and body and to do anything when you be most merry: but let your mirth be ever void of all scurrility and biting words to any man.

Three important events, of the little that is known, occurred in Sidney's boyhood:

He and Fulke Greville, who was afterwards to write so much and so movingly about him, entered Shrewsbury on the same day, in 1564.

In 1566, when he was twelve, he was presented with the poems of Virgil. And in the summer of that year he was summoned by his uncle, the Earl of Leicester and Chancellor of the University, to go from Shrewsbury to Oxford where he saw, for the first time, Queen Elizabeth in her, to his young eyes, uncomplicated glory.

Sidney, as a child, was of a charming and ingenuous appearance, as Thomas Moffett, in his recently discovered and translated *Nobilis* and *Lessus Lugubris*, testifies:

He was 'endowed with gifts of nature, with a strong and almost manly voice, and, in fine, with a certain consistent and absolute perfection of mind and body. When as a three year old he beheld the moon, with clean hands and head covered he used to pray to it and devoutly to worship.' Here follows the sonnet:

With how sad steps, ô Moone, thou clim'st the skyes,
    How silently, and with how wanne a face,
What may it be, that ev'n in heavenly place,

That busie Archer his sharpe Arrowes tryes?
Sure, if that long with love-acquainted eyes
    Can judge of love, thou feel'st a Lover's case,
    I reade within thy lookes thy languisht grace.
To mee, that feele the like, my state discries.
Then even of fellowship ô Moone tell me,
Is constant love deemde there but want of wit?
Are beauties there, as proude as heere they be?
Doe they above love to be lov'd, and yet
    Those Lovers scorne whom that love doth possesse?
    Doe they call vertue there ungratefulnesse?

The Earl of Leicester, then favoured by the queen, made sure that his nephew was a pretty boy to see her, bought him damask gowns trimmed with velvet, doublets of crimson and green taffeta, jerkins of blue leather, hose of carnation, shoes of white and green and blue. And he saw Elizabeth come into Oxford, clothed in scarlet silk and gold, with headdress of spun gold, her mantle of purple and ermine, and according to some historians, she sat on a high gold seat in an open litter drawn by mules.

In 1572, when he was eighteen, he received the queen's licence to undertake a two years' visit to the Continent.

Attached to the suite of the Earl of Lincoln, he went first to Paris: 'a grave and tender handsome youth,' or, as his uncle Leicester wrote in a letter to Walsingham, ambassador to France, 'young and raw.' A convinced and zealous Protestant by birth, education, and inclination, he was present at the anarchic eve of St Bartholomew's Day when an unknown number of thousands of

Protestants perished. At Frankfurt, he stayed at the shop of the scholarly printer, Andrew Wechel, where he met the learned Protestant controversialist, Hubert Languer, to whom, he confessed, he owed all his knowledge of literature and true religion. He visited Strasbourg, Vienna, Venice, Genoa, Florence, Padua (where he studied astronomy, geometry, music, and Greek), he travelled to Poland and came home. Leicester at once placed him at court, at Greenwich, where Elizabeth at the age of forty-two was, as Sidney wrote, 'somewhat advanced in years.' He was taught to be a courtier. He was at Kenilworth, in the dazzling, rippling, musical summer of 1575, where there were unforgettable pageants for the queen, masques and fireworks, the playing of gittern and cithern and virginals, tilts and jousts, bear-baiting, morris-dancing, tournaments, water-plays, and drinking from great livery pots of silver filled with claret and white wine.

In 1576, with the Earl of Essex, he joined his father in Ireland, and fought the boggish and cantankerous Irish who did not think, as he did, that English law was, in all the world, the most just and agreeable.

There Essex died, leaving a message for Sidney: 'Tell him I aned him nothing, but I wish him well, and so well that if God do move their hearts, I wish that he might match with my daughter. I call him son; he is so wise, so virtuous, and so godly; and if he go on in the course he hath begun, he will be as famous and worthy a gentleman as ever England bred.'

The daughter of Essex was Penelope Devereux, the Stella of the sonnets. Court life, home in England, proved expensive and lowering. His subsequent ambassadorship to the imperial court of Austria, splendid and unimportant. What he wanted, above all, was to serve the cause of Protestant religion. The queen allowed him no opportunities. His uncle, Leicester, was disgraced, almost fatally, by the queen's discovery of his hidden marriage. The queen herself was about to contract an unfortunate marriage with the house of Anjou. Sidney wrote to her his charming Discourse to the Queen's Majesty touching upon the affair and graciously attempting to dissuade her from it; for which he received no thanks. He challenged the unpleasant Earl of Oxford to a duel. John Stubbs, who had written a pamphlet expressing the feelings of the common people against Elizabeth's proposed marriage, had his offending right hand cut off with mallet and butcher's cleaver. And Sidney was, fortunately, so depressed by life in London, that he retired, from unemployment at court, to the company of his sister, the Countess of Pembroke, at Wilton House, in the Hundred of Branch and Dale, Wiltshire, there to write *Arcadia*.

Wilton was begun in the time of Henry VIII, under the conduct of Hans Holbein, and finished in the time of Edward VI for the first Earl of Pembroke. The garden of Wilton that Sir Philip Sidney knew and loved can be seen in an old print. Here are the embroidered plots with their four fountains; the plots of flowers, and beyond them the little terrace. Here are groves through which passes the river Nader, and statues of Bacchus and Flora, and covered arbours, and great ponds with fountains and columns and two crowns spinning on the top of the water; and a compartment of greens, and cherry-trees; and the great oval with the brass Gladiator; more arbours and turning galleries, porticos, and a terrace whose steps are sea-monsters.

Here was the most perfect house and garden for the writing of an Arcadian romance thronged with enchantments and disguised princes, murders, shepherds, sports, potions, and many kinds of love.

This enormously involved story, written in prose, and interspersed with songs and eclogues in verse, is dedicated 'To My Dear Lady and Sister, the Countess of Pembroke.'

'Here now have you (most dear, and most worthy to be the most dear Lady) this idle work of mine, which, I fear (like the spider's webbe) will be thought fitter to be swept away than worn to any other purpose.'

But here was no filigree web of words, but a huge tapestry woven to bewilder and to keep out the light. It is all ornament, spectacle and splendour, pageantry, pomp, and sumptuous profusion, frill, lace, gold and jewel, paradox, jingle, personification, descriptions of natural scenery and ethical reflections, battles, tournaments, sad shepherd's sheepish lyrics, all blurring beautifully and drowning at triumphal length.

He had written poetical theory, and now he tried his hand at poetical experiment, 'freely ranging within the Zodiack of his owne wit.'

The garlands hang their all too windy heads; the colours run and vanish; the cornucopia is full of holes; rhymes hang blowsy on the brow of the melting monument. How few the clear calm seconds in that rich desert of stationary time: these lines, perhaps, or are they too 'dainty'?

> The messenger made speed, and found Argalus at a castle of his own, sitting in a parlour with the fair Parthenia, he reading in a book the stories of Hercules,

> she by him, as to hear him read; but while his eyes looked on the book she looked on his eyes, and sometimes staying him with some pretty question, not so much to be resolved of the doubt as to give him occasion to look upon her. A happy couple, he joying in her, she joying in herself, but in herself because she enjoyed him.

And the famous description of the water-spaniel. And the eminently malicious line, interpreted by some critics as a statement of chivalrous loyalty: 'She was a queen, and therefore beautiful.'

But it is only in the sonnet sequence, *Astrophel and Stella*, that he is to be seen as a great poet. It was published five years after his death, in 1591. Nash says of it: 'This tragic-comedy of love is performed by star-light.'

The sonnets are addressed to Penelope Devereux, whose father wished Sidney to marry her. They begin with elegance and pretence, poems moving like courtiers dressed in the habit of love. They are *about* love, they are not *in* love; they *address* love, they do not speak *out* of it. The raptures are almost easily come by; the despair almost as easily relinquished. They are the most perfect exercises for a man about to be in love. And Penelope married, and Sidney had lost her, and the sonnets were no longer rehearsals for a poetic event but poetry itself, striding and burning:

> I might, unhappy word, (woe me) I might,
> And then would not, nor could not see my blisse:
> Tyll now, wrapt in a most infernall Night,
> I finde, how heavenly day (wretch) did I misse;
> Hart rent thy selfe, thou doost thy selfe but right.

No lovely Paris made thy Helen his,
No force, no fraude, rob'd thee of thy delight,
No Fortune of thy fortune Author is;
But to my selfe, my selfe did give the blow,
While too much wit forsooth so troubled me,
That I respects for both our sakes must showe.
And could I not by rysing morne for-see,
How faire a day was neere, (ô punisht eyes)
That I had beene more foolish, or more wise.

In these sonnets we see, held still in time for us, a whole progress of passion, physical and spiritual, coursing through rage and despair, self-pity, hope renewed, exultancy, moon-moved dreams, black fear, and blinding bright certainty of final loss.

There are several songs among the sonnets. In the eighth song, Stella gently kills his hope of possessing her.

In a grove most rich of shade;
Where birds wanton Musicke made;
Maie then young his pide weeds shewing,
New perfumes with flowrs fresh growing. . . .

In the storming of Zutphen in the Netherlands, October the second, 1586, Sir Philip Sidney was struck by a musket-ball in the thigh. On his agonized way back to the camp, 'being thirsty with excess of bleeding, he called for a drink, which was presently brought him; but, as he was putting the bottle to his mouth, he saw a poor soldier carried along, who had eaten his last at the same feast, ghastly casting up his eyes at the bottle, which Sir Philip, perceiving, took it from his head before he drank, and delivered it to the poor man with these words, "Thy necessity is yet greater than mine."'

The operations upon his wound were long and painful. 'When they began to dress his wound, he, both by way of charge and advice, told them that while his strength was still entire, his body free from fever, and his mind able to endure, they might freely use their art, cut, and search to the bottom.'

They used their art, and he was taken away to Arnhem. There he suffered. He became a mere skeleton. The shoulder-bones broke through the skin.

'He one morning lifting up the clothes for change and ease of his body, smelt some extraordinary noisome savour about him, differing from oils and salves, as he conceived.' Mortification had set in.

Eight days after he was wounded, he sent for ministers of many nationalities, and they prayed with him.

He asked for music.

He dictated his will.

He wrote a long letter in Latin.

He bade good-bye to his brother.

Very near death, he said: 'I would not change my joy for the empire of the world.'

A Dearth of Comic Writers

The condition of the world *to-day* is such that most writers feel they cannot truthfully be 'comic' about it. (Was the world ever such that they could?) Perhaps they say: Can we single out the amiably comic eccentricity of individual beings, the ludicrous, the *gauche*, the maximless gawky, the dear and the daft and the droll, the runcible Booby, the Toby, the Pickwick, the barmy old Adam, when daily we are confronted, as social beings, by the delt and the peeve and the minge and the bully, the maniac new Atom? I prefer the attitude of Pepys: '12th, Friday. Up, finding our beds good, but lousy; which made us merry' . . .

Comic writers can't expect society to be comic just for *them*. 'Do you serve women at this bar?' 'No,' says the barman, 'you've got to bring your own.' And society to a comic writer is always funny, even, or especially, on its death-bed. People walking into open lift shafts, being wolfed by lions, missing the swung trapeze, are conventional subjects for a comic draughtsman; and the sight of society falling on its ear, and the prospect of civilization itself going for a burton, offer writers possibilities of every kind of laugh. 'There is something in the house,' said the wife of a comic writer, in one of Algernon Blackwood's *John Silence* stories, 'that prevents his feeling funny.' There's enough, God knows, going on in *our* house to drive Peacock's Prince Seithennyn from drink; but that doesn't prevent a writer from creating a great comic world of his own out of the tragic catastrophe of this. 'The best lack all conviction, while the worst are full of passionate intensity,' wrote Yeats. But grave, censorious, senatorial, soul-possessing Man, erect on his two spindles, is still a colossal joke. A man in love makes a practical cat laugh. A man in power makes Engels weep—with laughter . . .

[*W. W. Jacobs was*] one of the trimmest, funniest, and most exact Edwardian writers, whose dialogue is as neat and sly and spare and taut as his mercenary and matrimonial plots. Here, in what I call a *minor* comic world, are the landlubber dreams of sailors-on-leave, the visions of a pocketful of Bradburys in snug saloons with buxom barmaids. Here are the intricate discomfitures of rival seamen; truculent unpaid rolling-pinned landladies; free fills of baccy; beer on the sly and the nod and the slate. Here all married women are harridans, all widows are plump and comfy and have a little bit put by, all unmarried girls are arch and mysterious, all men without exception are knaves and fools, and very often both, and are solely occupied in strategies concerning money and women and the getting and losing of them.

[*Speaking of Stephen Leacock's works he said:*] I read only his *Sunshine Sketches of a Little Town*, for only in these did Leacock create a *home* for his imagination, a 'place' in which *his* people could be born and die, love, fall down, philosophize, have their hair cut, let their hair down, put their feet up.

[*Calder Marshall asked:*] Doesn't P. G. Wodehouse fit your definition of a comic world perfectly?

[*Thomas replied:*] Those chinless, dim eyeglassed, asinine, bespatted drones were borrowed, lock, stock, and title, from memories of the Pink 'Un period and the Smart Set, from the ghostly, hansom past of the moneyed masher and the stage-door johnny. Some people like Jeeves, but include me out: I, for one, do not appreciate gentleman's gentleman's relish.

A truly comic, invented world must live *at the same time* as the world *we* live in.

What does [*present day comic writing*] amount to? Funny columns in English newspapers, fence-sittings, beachcombings, shymakings; the laboured, witless whimsy and pompous facetiousness of that national institution—or poorhouse of ideas—which the *New Yorker* once called 'Paunch.' All the best *books*—or nearly all the best modern comic books are written by Americans.

James Thurber, S. J. Perelman, Frank Sullivan, and Robert Benchley, all *have* written for that brilliant family magazine, but have nothing in common except their superiority to modern English comic journalists.

[*It is*] still impossible to compare the shy and baffled, introspective essays, fables, and fabulous reminiscences of Thurber, his cowering terror before the mechanical gadgets, the militant neuroses, the ubiquitous women, the democratic pitfalls and big-business bogies of this modern Americanized Age, it's impossible to compare him, class him, school him, with the glib Groucho zaniness of S. J. Perelman, who writes like a Hollywood advertising copywriter after reading James Joyce, Amanda Ross, Kraft-Ebbing, Doctor Spooner, E. E. Cummings, and Sam Goldwyn's ace publicity stooge in a state of hypertension in a Turkish bath managed by Man-Mountain Dean. But Thurber, Sullivan, Perelman, Benchley, all excellent comic writers, are all *essayists*;

and I am concerned with comic, constructive writers of *stories*. I want, without boisterous backslapping, without the hail-fellow guffaw of the tweedy pipe-sucking tankard-quaffing professional literary comedian, without nudge and titter, without the reedy neigh of the reviewer, I want laughter in books, the sight and smell and *sound* of laughter. And almost the only sound I hear from stories now recalls, to me, the sound of the watch in Frances Cornford's poem:

I thought it said in every tick;
I am so sick, so sick, so sick;
O death, come quick, come quick, come quick,
Come quick, come quick, come quick, come quick.

The English Festival of Spoken Poetry

There is, in many people, a need to share enthusiasm, which is often expressed in behaviour known, nicely, as 'showing off'; common to actors, poets, politicians, and other trapezists. Many people who read poems like some of them so much that they cannot keep their liking to themselves: they are not content with saying, 'Do you know de la Eliot's "Waste Stranger" or W. H. Housman's "A Dog Beneath the Gallows." Isn't it, or aren't they, lovely,' but they needs must say 'Listen to this,' and reel the lovely stuff off aloud. Sometimes they like the noise their voices make. They find that the words of the poem they reel, familiar and pleasant, acquire a surprising pleasant strangeness when boomed, minced, Keened, crooned, Dyalled, or Wolfitted. Known words grow wings; print springs and shoots; the voice discovers the poet's ear; it's found that a poem on a page is only half a poem. And the speakers, realizing the inadequacy of their hitherto silent interpretation, sometimes set about learning the business of reading aloud; which is to say, they set about learning the poems which they know by heart, by head and tongue. They put that noise on paper, which is a poem, into their chests and throats, and let it out: they find that good poets are better than they (the readers) thought they were, for crying out loud. And then some of these readers, wanting to show others all that is missed by reading poetry dumb, look around for an audience. Families, like countries, take their prophets unkindly, but a verse-speaker in the home is dishonour to be hooted. Show me the family circle that sits in silence while a son or daughter mouths, with gawky zeal, a lyric aloud, and I will recite the whole of *Hudibras* to a week-end convention of Moose. These readers cannot rush into the Third Programme at a moment's notice, past the sentinel guard of artists' rifles, disturb the uneven tenor of Tibetan operas and the phalanx of harpsichords. They can found verse-speaking societies in their home places, but who is there to listen except other verse-readers who are only waiting for them to stop? Where can people who like reading poems aloud very much do it? Do it, that is, to a discriminating, enthusiastic, and, on the whole, altruistic audience?

The Oxford Festival of Spoken Poetry was founded twenty years ago, and grew up around the love and care of the late Laurence Binyon. The festival took place in Oxford until the outbreak of the last never-to-be-repeated war. Now it is conducted in London, but its committee and their supporters hope soon to be able to return to Oxford. The Festival of Spoken Poetry is run by poets. Nearly all the judges are poets; poets; men who work hard at another job in order to be able to work hard at the job they really like when they're not working. The judges of the festival: cool (specially now), impersonal, knowledgeable, mature, lofty uncompromising not-to-be-bribed-or-trifled-with ascetic remote creatures who (if only the competitors could know—and I speak for the masculine judges alone) sit there in their perspiring glory, thinking of cricket and ice and legs, their little hearts thumping among so many summery flowered dresses, bright smiles, untrammelled youth, high heels, endeavour, scent, and zeal.

It may perhaps be thought that I am frivolling about what is, really, a most sincere, conscientious, and extremely able festival. But it *is* a festival. It is not a cold competition. It runs for four days every year, and it is to be enjoyed. We all enjoy it, competitors, judges, carpers, audience, and all. There were over 300 people this year, from all over the country, who stood up and read Marlowe, Tennyson, Sydney Keyes, Pope, mostly because they love reading poems aloud and here was the place and the time to read them with no strings or nonsense. This is no Phil the High-Falutin's Ball, but a festival of and for unfrumpish, unfreakish, sane people with voices. When a competitor is not reading, he or she is listening to the others read: and listening with a knowledgeable liking.

I'm not going to say that all the readers are first class. This is a festival and an amateur competition, not a professional day out for successful exhibitionists. Many of the competitors would wish to become full-time actors, readers, broadcasters; a few may be. Like everything that is any good, this festival is full of faults. I think that the readers should be allowed, if they want to, to have, in front of them, the text of the poems they are reading. I thought that when a *long* poem came up to be read, some of the competitors very dully over-slowed their reading because they had too much to remember and were, all too obviously, feeling for the next verse. I thought that some of the 'judgments' had to be made too hastily, so that a tepid, but finished, reading was likely to be valued higher than a true, warm but hesitant, occasionally blundering, one.

Many readings were plagued with the more obvious sicknesses of reading aloud: insistent sibilance, the, for want of a better phrase, 'Old Vic' voice: an affected inflecting that strangles rhythm and truncheons meaning. There was the 'dead voice': a way of speaking that pretends to emphasize the importance of flat understatement only because the ability to *give* isn't there. The smile, not the voice, beautiful: the supposition of an arch, nudging connivance between speaker and listener; the attitude of '*We* know, though the others don't.' There was, though rarely, the *acting* of the spoken word, the taught, but never taut, gesture to illustrate an unillustratable, except by inflexion, point or temper of a line, the starry-eyed horizon-searching, the mechanical handwork of simulated passion, like a soprano milking a goat.

But oh so rare. Nearly everyone, nearly *everyone*, enjoyed this festival as it has been enjoyed for twenty years. No humbug. No Slade-fringed or tennis-party voice, no hairy crank with a jaegar lilt or a maypole accent, no henna'd and bangled New-lifing. And the standard of the reading was extremely high. Poems are written in lines, and if you shut your eyes, which was sometimes difficult to do, you could hear, with no jarring of brakes, where the lines stopped. You could *hear*.

On Reading One's Own Poems

To choose what I should read to-night, I looked through seventy odd poems of mine, and found that many *are* odd indeed and that some may be poems. And I decided not to choose those that strike me, still, as pretty peculiar, but to stick to a few of the ones that do move a little way towards the state and destination I imagine I intended to be theirs when, in small rooms in Wales, arrogantly and devotedly I began them.

For I like to think that the poems most narrowly odd are among those I wrote earliest, and that the later poems are wider and deeper—though Time, if interested, may well prove me wrong, and find that the reverse is true, or that each statement is false.

I do not remember—that is the point—the first impulse that pumped and shoved most of the earlier poems along, and they are still too near to me, with their vehement beat-pounding black and green rhythms like those of a very young policeman exploding, for me to see the written evidence of it. My interpretation of them—if that is not too weighty a word just for reading them aloud and trying to give some idea of their sound and shape—could only be a parroting of the say that I once had.

'And all that a reader-aloud of his own poems can hope to do is to try to put across his own memory of the original impulses behind his poems, deepening, maybe, and if only for a moment, the inner meaning of the words on the printed pages.'

How I wish I could agree whole-heartedly with that, let alone hope to achieve it! But, oh, the danger! For what a reader-aloud of his own poems so often does, is to mawken or melodramatize them, making a single simple phrase break with the fears or throb with the terrors from which he deludes himself the phrase has been born.

There is the other reader, of course, who manages, by studious flatness, semi-detachment, and an almost condescending undersaying of his poems, to give the impression that what he really means is: Great things, but my own.

That I belong to the very *dangerous* first group of readers will be only too clear.

The first poem is titled by its first line: 'There Was a Saviour.'

There was a saviour
Rarer than radium,
Commoner than water, crueller than truth;
Children kept from the sun
Assembled at his tongue
To hear the golden note turn in a groove,
Prisoners of wishes locked their eyes
In the jails and studies of his keyless smiles.

The voice of children says
From a lost wilderness
There was calm to be done in his safe unrest,
When hindering man hurt

Man, animal, or bird
We hid our fears in that murdering breath,
Silence, silence to do, when earth grew loud,
In lairs and asylums of the tremendous shout.

There was glory to hear
In the churches of his tears,
Under his downy arm you sighed as he struck,
O you who could not cry
On to the ground when a man died
Put a tear for joy in the unearthly flood
And laid your cheek against a cloud-formed shell:
Now in the dark there is only yourself and myself.

Two proud, blacked brothers cry,
Winter-locked side by side,
To this inhospitable hollow year,
O we who could not stir
One lean sigh when we heard
Greed on man beating near and fire neighbour
But wailed and nested in the sky-blue wall
Now break a giant tear for the little known fall,

For the drooping of homes
That did not nurse our bones,
Brave deaths of only ones but never found,
Now see, alone in us,
Our own true strangers' dust
Ride through the doors of our unentered house.
Exiled in us we arouse the soft,
Unclenched, armless, silk and rough love that breaks all
rocks.

The next poem tells of a mother and her child who is about to be born. It is not a narrative, nor an argument, but a series of conflicting images which move through pity and violence to an unreconciled acceptance of suffering: the mother's *and* the child's. This poem has been called obscure. I refuse to believe that it is obscurer than pity, violence, or suffering. But being a poem, not a lifetime, it is more compressed:

'If my head hurt a hair's foot
Pack back the downed bone. If the unpricked ball of my breath
Bump on a spout let the bubbles jump out.
Sooner drop with the worm of the ropes round my throat
Than bully ill love in the clouted scene.

'All game phrases fit your ring of a cockfight:
I'll comb the snared woods with a glove on a lamp,
Peck, sprint, dance on fountains and duck time
Before I rush in a crouch the ghost with a hammer, air,
Strike light, and bloody a loud room.

'If my bunched, monkey coming is cruel
Rage me back to the making house. My hand unravel
When you sew the deep door. The bed is a cross place.
Bend, if my journey ache, direction like an arc or make
A limp and riderless shape to leap nine thinning months.'

'No. Not for Christ's dazzling bed
Or a nacreous sleep among soft particles and charms
My dear would I change my tears or your iron head.
Thrust, my daughter or son, to escape, there is none, none, none,
Nor when all ponderous heaven's host of waters breaks.

'Now to awake husked of gestures and my joy like a cave
To the anguish and carrion, to the infant forever unfree,
O my lost love bounced from a good home;
The grain that hurries this way from the rim of the grave
Has a voice and a house, and there and here you must couch and cry.

'Rest beyond choice in the dust-appointed grain,
At the breast stored with seas. No return
Through the waves of the fat streets nor the skeleton's thin ways.
The grave and my calm body are shut to your coming as stone,
And the endless beginning of prodigies suffers open.'

Reading one's own poems aloud is letting the cat out of the bag. You may have always suspected bits of a poem to be overweighted, overviolent, or daft, and then, suddenly, with the poet's tongue around them, your suspicion is made certain. How he slows up a line to savour it, remembering what trouble it took, once upon a time, to make it just so, at the very moment, you may think, when the poem needs crispness and speed. Does the cat snarl or mew the better when its original owner—or father, even, the tom-poet—let it out of the bag, than when another does, who never put it in?

It was my thirtieth year to heaven
Woke to my hearing from harbour and neighbour wood
And the mussel pooled and the heron
Priested shore
The morning beckon
With water praying and call of seagull and rook
And the knock of sailing boats on the net webbed wall
Myself to set foot
That second
In the still sleeping town and set forth.

My birthday began with the water-
Birds and the birds of the winged trees flying my name
Above the farms and the white horses
And I rose
In rainy autumn
And walked abroad in a shower of all my days.
High tide and the heron dived when I took the road
Over the border
And the gates
Of the town closed as the town awoke.

A springful of larks in a rolling
Cloud and the roadside bushes brimming with whistling
Blackbirds and the sun of October
Summery
On the hill's shoulder,
Here were fond climates and sweet singers suddenly
Come in the morning where I wandered and listened
To the rain wringing
Wind blow cold
In the wood faraway under me.

Pale rain over the dwindling harbour
And over the sea wet church the size of a snail
With its horns through mist and the castle
Brown as owls
But all the gardens
Of spring and summer were blooming in the tall tales
Beyond the border and under the lark full cloud.
There could I marvel
My birthday
Away but the weather turned around.

It turned away from the blithe country
And down the other air and the blue altered sky
Streamed again a wonder of summer
With apples
Pears and red currants
And I saw in the turning so clearly a child's
Forgotten mornings when he walked with his mother
Through the parables
Of sun light
And the legends of the green chapels

And the twice told fields of infancy
That his tears burned my cheeks and his heart moved in mine.
These were the woods the river and sea
Where a boy
In the listening
Summertime of the dead whispered the truth of his joy
To the trees and the stones and the fish in the tide.
And the mystery
Sang alive
Still in the water and singingbirds.

And there could I marvel my birthday
Away but the weather turned around. And the true
Joy of the long dead child sang burning
In the sun.
It was my thirtieth
Year to heaven stood there then in the summer noon
Though the town below lay leaved with October blood.
O may my heart's truth
Still be sung
On this high hill in a year's turning.

The next poem I'll read is the only one I have written that is, directly, about the life and death of one particular human being I knew—and not about the very many lives and deaths whether seen, as in my first poems, in the tumultous world of my own being or, as in the later poems, in war, grief, and the great holes and corners of universal love.

After the funeral, mule praises, brays,
Windshake of sailshaped ears, muffle-toed tap
Tap happily of one peg in the thick
Grave's foot, blinds down the lids, the teeth in black,
The spittled eyes, the salt ponds in the sleeves,
Morning smack of the spade that wakes up sleep,
Shakes a desolate boy who slits his throat
In the dark of the coffin and sheds dry leaves,
That breaks one bone to light with a judgment clout,
After the feast of tear-stuffed time and thistles
In a room with a stuffed fox and a stale fern,
I stand, for this memorial's sake, alone
In the snivelling hours with dead, humped Ann

Whose hooded, fountain heart once fell in puddles
Round the parched worlds of Wales and drowned each
sun
(Though this for her is a monstrous image blindly
Magnified out of praise; her death was a still drop;
She would not have me sinking in the holy
Flood of her heart's fame; she would lie dumb and deep
And need no druid of her broken body).
But I, Ann's bard on a raised hearth, call all
The seas to service that her wood-tongued virtue
Babble like a bellbuoy over the hymning heads,
Bow down the walls of the ferned and foxy woods
That her love sing and swing through a brown chapel,
Bless her bent spirit with four, crossing birds.
Her flesh was meek as milk, but this skyward statue
With the wild breast and blessed and giant skull
Is carved from her in a room with a wet window
In a fiercely mourning house in a crooked year.
I know her scrubbed and sour humble hands
Lie with religion in their cramp, her threadbare
Whisper in a damp word, her wits drilled hollow,
Her fist of a face died clenched on a round pain;
And sculptured Ann is seventy years of stone.
These cloud-sopped, marble hands, this monumental
Argument of the hewn voice, gesture and psalm,
Storm me forever over her grave until
The stuffed lung of the fox twitch and cry Love
And the strutting fern lay seeds on the black sill.

Welsh Poets

The position—if poets must have positions, other than upright—of the poet born in Wales or of Welsh parentage and writing his poems in English is to-day made by many people unnecessarily, and trivially, difficult. There is a number of young Welshmen writing poems in English, who, insisting passionately that they are Welshmen, should by rights, be writing in Welsh, but who, unable to write in Welsh or reluctant to do so because of the uncommercial nature of the language, often give the impression that their writing in English is only a condescension to the influence and ubiquity of a tyrannous foreign tongue. I do not belong to that number. . . .

There are not more than half a dozen Welsh poets who wrote in English of any genuine importance between 1622, when Henry Vaughan was born, and 1944, when Alun Lewis died, though there are many able and charming writers. All I can say . . . is that Welshmen have written, from time to time, exceedingly good poetry in English. I should like to think that that is because they were, and are, good poets rather than good Welshmen. It's the poetry, written in the language which is most natural to the poet, that counts, not his continent, country, island, race, class, or political persuasion.

Henry Vaughan

Before [*Henry Vaughan there*] was a magnificent tradition of poetry in the Welsh language. Dafydd ap Gwilym, for instance, a contemporary of Chaucer, is thought, by most Celtic scholars, to be as good a poet.

Vaughan, who belonged to a very ancient Welsh family and who was educated in England, must surely have known ap Gwilym's poems. But he certainly did not follow in the exuberant bardsmanship of that great court poet but derived, in the first place, his style and matter from George Herbert. He wrote in a time when one poet *could* derive manner and content from another and yet be original. He read, too, and loved, the poetry of John Donne, but he loved it most as he saw it reflected, and transmuted, in the work of Herbert. The world, to Vaughan, was 'no less than a veil of the Eternal Spirit, whose presence may be felt in any, and the smallest part.' Readers to-day may prefer him not as a mystical theologist but as a wonderful poet of pieces: a magician of intervals. They remember odd lines, rather than odder poems. They think, perhaps of this, from a poem on the Grave:

> A nest of nights, a gloomy sphere,
> Where shadows thicken, and the cloud
> Sits on the Sun's brow all the year,
> And nothing moves without a shroud.

Or a single image:

> . . . stars nod and sleep
> And through the dark air spin a fiery thread.

Or, again, from the 'Day-Spring':

> Early, while yet the dark was gay,
> And gilt with stars more trim than day.
> Heaven's Lily and the Earth's chaste Rose,
> The green, immortal Branch arose,
> And in a solitary place
> Bowed to his father His blessed face.

And, of the many superb opening lines:

I saw Eternity the other night,
Like a great ring of pure and endless light.

But I have chosen one whole poem, 'The Night,' in which the figures of his authentic and intense vision move across a wild, and yet inevitably ordered, sacred landscape.

Through that pure virgin-shrine,
That sacred veil drawn o'er Thy glorious noon,
That men might look and live, as glow-worms shine,
And face the moon:
Wise Nicodemus saw such light
As made him know his God by night.

Most blest believer he!
Who in that land of darkness and blind eyes
Thy long expected healing wings could see,
When Thou didst rise,
And what can never more be done,
Did at midnight speak with the sun!

O who will tell me, where
He found Thee at that dead and silent hour!
What hallow'd solitary ground did bear
So rare a flower,
Within whose sacred leaves did lie
The fullness of the Deity.

No mercy-seat of gold,
No dead and dusty cherub, nor carv'd stone,
But His own living works did my Lord hold
And lodge alone;
Where trees and herbs did watch and peep
And wonder, while the Jews did sleep.

Dear night! this world's defeat;
The stop to busy fools; care's check and curb;
The day of spirits; my soul's calm retreat
Which none disturb!
CHRIST's progress, and His prayer time;
The hours to which high heaven doth chime.

God's silent searching flight:
When my Lord's head is fill'd with dew, and all
His locks are wet with the clear drops of night;
His still, soft call;
His knocking time; the soul's dumb watch,
When spirits their fair kindred catch.

Were all my loud, evil days
Calm and unhaunted as in thy dark tent,
Whose peace but by some angel's wing or voice
Is seldom rent;
Then I in Heaven all the long year
Would keep, and never wander here.

But living where the sun
Doth all things wake, and where all mix and tire
Themselves and others, I consent and run
To ev'ry mire,
And by this world's ill-guiding light,
Err more than I can do by night.

There is in GOD (some say)
A deep, but dazzling darkness; as men here
Say it is late and dusky, because they
See not all clear;
O for that Night! where I in Him
Might live invisible and dim!

Edward Thomas

From Edward Thomas, who was killed in France in 1917, to Alun Lewis, who died in India in 1944, there sprang into life a whole new body of poetry written by Welshmen. I do not think that there was in common between these poets anything but a love of poetry and of their own country. They did not, to any marked degree, derive from the same poetical sources. Edward Thomas, for instance, was devoted, through all his pitifully short, and too often melancholy, life, to the most English work of Thomas Hardy, John Clare the Northamptonshire peasant, and William Barnes the Dorset poet. He loved always the rich brown stables and paddocks of the painter George Morland and the loving landscapes of old Crome. He loved the fields, the woods, the winding roads, he knew a thousand country things: the diamonds of rain on the grassblades, the ghostly white parsley flower, mouse and wren and robin, each year's first violets, the missel-thrush that loves juniper, hawthorn berry, hazel-tuft, new-mown hay, the cuckoo crying over the untouched dew, churches, graveyards, farms and byres, children, wild geese, horses in the sun. In the words of Walter de la Mare, Edward Thomas was a faithful and solitary lover of the lovely that is not beloved by most of us, at much expense. And when, indeed, he was killed in Flanders, a mirror of England was shattered of so pure and true a crystal that a clearer and tenderer reflection can be found no other where than in these poems.

Here is a poem of his written in Wales.

Mother, the root of this little yellow flower
Among the stones has the taste of quinine.
Things are strange to-day on the cliff. The sun shines
so bright,
And the grasshopper works at his sewing-machine
So hard. Here's one on my hand, mother, look;
I lie so still. There's one on your book.

But I have something to tell more strange. So leave
Your book to the grasshopper, mother dear,—
Like a green knight in a dazzling market-place,—
And listen now. Can you hear what I hear
Far out? Now and then the foam there curls
And stretches a white arm out like a girl's.

Fishes and gulls ring no bells. There cannot be
A chapel or church between here and Devon,
With fishes or gulls ringing its bell,—hark!—
Somewhere under the sea or up in heaven.
'It's the bell, my son, out in the bay
On the buoy. It does sound sweet to-day.'

Sweeter I never heard, mother, no, not in all Wales.
I should like to be lying under that foam,
Dead, but able to hear the sound of the bell,
And certain that you would often come
And rest, listening happily.
I should be happy if that could be.

W. H. Davies

W. H. Davies (1871–1940) was born in Monmouthshire and apprenticed, very early, to a picture-frame maker. He tramped through America as a hobo, crossed the Atlantic many times on cattle boats, and was a pedlar and street singer in England. Utterly poor and alone, educated by chance reading in the slums of great cities, he began, suddenly, to write verse which was in the direct tradition of Robert Herrick. From the very beginning to the end, during which he wrote voluminously, his poems were always fresh and simple and assured. There was inevitability in his slightest verses; unique observation in his tiniest reflections on the natural world.

His most famous poems are about birds and clouds and animals, the journeying of the planets and the seasons, the adventure of the coming and going of simple night and day. But I have chosen two of his more unfamiliar poems, which will perhaps show him, to many, in a strange new light, but in a light no less scrupulously fair and loving than that in which his kingfishers, his robin-redbreasts, the little hunchbacks in the snow, all the inhabitants of his small and pure world move about their mysterious errands in the sky and on the earth he so much loved.

(*The Inquest*)

I took my oath I would inquire
  Without affection, hate, or wrath,
Into the death of Ada Wright—
  So help me God! I took that oath.

When I went out to see the corpse,
  The four months' babe that died so young,
I judged it was seven pounds in weight,
  And little more than one foot long.

One eye, that had a yellow lid,
  Was shut—so was the mouth, that smiled;
The left eye open, shining bright—
  It seemed a knowing little child.

For as I looked at that one eye,
  It seemed to laugh, and say with glee:
'What caused my death you'll never know—
  Perhaps my mother murdered me.'

When I went into court again,
  To hear the mother's evidence—
It was a love-child, she explained,
  And smiled, for our intelligence.

'Now, Gentlemen of the Jury,' said
  The coroner—'this woman's child
By misadventure met its death.'
  'Aye, aye' said we. The mother smiled.

And I could see that child's one eye
  Which seemed to laugh, and say with glee:
'What caused my death you'll never know—
  Perhaps my mother murdered me.'

(*The Bust*)

When I went wandering far from home,
I left a woman in my room
To clean my hearth and floor, and dust
My shelves and pictures, books and bust.

When I came back a welcome glow
Burned in her eyes—her voice was low;
And everything was in its place,
As clean and bright as her own face.

But when I looked more closely there,
The dust was on my dark, bronze hair;
The nose and eyebrows too were white—
And yet the lips were clean and bright.

The years have gone, and so has she,
But still the truth remains with me—
How that hard mouth was once kept clean
By living lips that kissed unseen.

Idris Davies

W. H. Davies lived much of his life in poverty, and in sickening surroundings. It never made him angry, at least not in his poems. But out of the mining valleys of South Wales, there were poets who were beginning to write in a spirit of passionate anger against the inequality of social conditions. They wrote, not of the truths and beauties of the natural world, but of the lies and ugliness of the unnatural system of society under which they worked—or, more often during the nineteen-twenties and thirties, under which they were not allowed to work. They spoke, in ragged and angry rhythms, of the Wales *they* knew: the coal-tips, the dole-queues, the stubborn bankrupt villages, the children, scrutting for coal on the slag-heaps, the colliers' shabby allotments, the cheap-jack cinema, the whippet races, the disused quarries, the still pit-wheels, the gaunt tin-roofed chapels in the soot, the hewers squatting in the cut, the pubs, the Woolworths, the deacons and the gyppos, silicosis, little Moscow up beyond the hills, sag-roof factory and plumeless stack, stone-grey street, scummed river, the capped and mufflered knots of men outside the grim employment exchange and the public library. Among these poets, Idris Davies is perhaps the only one who has attempted to shape his violence into real poems, and he often achieves a lyrical simplicity which in no way lessens the intensity of his hatred of injustice. In some of his poems he can even bring himself to write with a kind of sad and jaunty happiness about his people and his country, as in

'He won't talk any more of the distant days . . .'

And Idris Davies has written, too, in *Gwalia Deserta*, one very simple and moving song—

O what can you give me?
Say the sad bells of Rhymney.

Is there hope for the future?
Cry the brown bells of Merthyr.

Who made the mineowner?
Say the black bells of Rhondda.

And who robbed the miner?
Cry the grim bells of Blaina.

They will plunder willy-nilly,
Say the bells of Caerphilly.

They have fangs, they have teeth!
Shout the loud bells of Neath.

To the south, things are sullen,
Say the pink bells of Brecon.

Even God is uneasy,
Say the moist bells of Swansea.

Put the vandals in court!
Cry the bells of Newport.

All would be well if—if—if—
Say the green bells of Cardiff.

Why so worried, sisters, why?
Sing the silver bells of Wye.

Glyn Jones

Glyn Jones, now a schoolmaster, is one of the few young Welshmen writing English poetry to-day who has a deep knowledge of *Welsh* poetry itself, and he has tried, in several English poems, to use the very difficult ancient bardic forms. These forms rely on a great deal of assonance and alliteration and most complicated internal rhyming; and these effects in English have, in the hands of the few who have attempted to use them, succeeded only in warping, crabbing, and obscuring the natural genius of the English language. But, when Glyn Jones is not experimenting in what must always be, to ears accustomed to English poetry, unavoidably awkward sound and syntax, he can write as surely as this. The poem, in which I think you will be able to detect, straight away, the influence of D. H. Lawrence, especially in the last stanza, is called 'Esyllt.'

As he climbs down our hill, my kestrel rises,
Steering in silence up from five empty fields,
A smooth sun brushed brown across his shoulders,
Floating in wide circles, his warm wings stiff.
Their shadows cut; in new soft orange hunting boots
My lover crashes through the snapping bracken.

The still gorse-hissing hill burns, brags gold broom's
Outcropping quartz; each touched bush spills dew.
Strangely, last moment's parting was never sad,
But unreal, like my promised years; less felt
Than this intense and silver snail calligraphy
Scrawled here in the sun across these stones.

Why have I often wanted to cry out
More against his going when he has left my flesh
Only for the night? When he has gone out
Hot from my mother's kitchen, and my combs
Were on the table under the lamp, and the wind
Was banging the doors of the shed in the yard.

Alun Lewis

Alun Lewis was killed by accident, while serving in India, in 1944. Three of the very finest—perhaps *the* very finest it will be found, in another and a quieter day—of the poets who wrote in the two Great Wars of this century were Edward Thomas, Wilfred Owen, and Alun Lewis. Thomas and Owen were twenty-five years of age; Lewis, twenty-eight. All three were Welshmen. I have no comment, of any national reference, to add to that. Lewis was a healer and an illuminator, humble before his own confessions, awed before the eternal confession of love by the despised and condemned inhabitants of the world crumbling around him. He wrote:

> I have no more desire to express
> The old relationships, of love fulfilled
> Or stultified, capacity for pain,
> Nor to say gracefully all that the poets have said
> Of one or other of the old compulsions,
> For now the times are gathered for confession.

And, always, humbly, never as a priest but as a servant, he heard them. He knew, like Wilfred Owen, that, in war, the poetry is in the pity. And, like Owen, he could never place himself above pity but must give it tongue, as in this extract from an unfinished play in which Sacco, the comrade of Vanzetti, writes from prison to his son:

> And for yourself, remember in the play
> Of happiness you must not act alone.
> The joy is in the sharing of the feast.
> Also be like a man in how you greet

The suffering that makes your young face thin.
Be not perturbed if you are called to fight.
Only a fool thinks life was made his way,
A fool or the daughter of a wealthy house.

Husband yourself, but never stale your mind
With prudence or with doubting. I could wish
You saw my body slipping from the chair
To-morrow. You'd remember that, my son,
And would not weigh the cost of our struggle
Against the product as a poor wife does.
But I'll not break your sleep with such a nightmare.
You looked so happy when you lay asleep . . .

But I have neither strength nor room for all
These thoughts. One single thought's enough
To fill immensity. I drop my pen . . .
I hope this letter finds you in good health,
My son, my comrade. Will you give my love
To Inez and your mother and my friends.
Bartolo also sends his greetings to you.
I would have written better and more simple
Except my head spins like a dancing top
And my hand trembles. . . . I am Oh, so weak . . .

Wales and the Artist

Too many of the artists of Wales who go to live permanently in, for example, London, begin almost at once to anglicize themselves beyond recognition (though this, of course, does not apply to artists alone. I know in London a Welsh hairdresser who has striven so vehemently to abolish his accent that he sounds like a man speaking with the Elgin Marbles in his mouth). They ape the narrow 'a.' They repudiate the Welsh language, whether they know it or not. By the condescending telling of comic apocryphal tales about Dai and Evan from the valleys, they earn, in the company of cultural lickspittles who condescend to them in their turn, sorry dinners and rounds of flat drinks. They fall for the latest 'isms' gullibly as pups for rubber bones. They confirm, by their spaniel adulation and their ignorance of the tradition that inevitably leads to the experiment, the suspicions of un-Welsh experimental artists that all the Welsh are humbugs, especially Welsh artists. In exhibitions, concerts, cocktail parties, there they are on the horn-rimmed edges, stifling their natural ardour so that they may disparagingly drawl, and with knowledgeable satiety, of the paintings, the music, the guests, their host, corseting their voices so that no lilt or inflection of Welsh enthusiasm may exult or pop out. 'Ectually,' they say, 'I was born in Cwmbwrla, but Soho's better for my *gouaches*.' They set up, in grey, whining London, a little mock Wales of their own, an exile government of dispossessed intellectuals dispossessed not of their country but of their intellects. And they return home, every long now and then, like slummers, airily to treat and backslap their grooved old friends, to inquire, half-laughingly, the whereabouts of streets and buildings as though they did not know them in the deepest dark, to drag, with all the magnets of their snobbery, the Christian names and numbers of wives of aged painters, the haunts of up-and-going poets, the intimate behaviour of the famous musicians whom they have not met, and to jingle in their pockets and mouths their foreign-made pennies, opinions, and intonations.

On the other hand, too many of the artists of Wales stay in Wales too long, giants in the dark behind the parish pump, pygmies in the nationless sun, enviously sniping at the artists of other countries rather than attempting to raise the standard of art of their own country by working fervently at their own words, paint, or music.

And too many of the artists of Wales spend too much time talking about the position of the artists of Wales.

There is only one position for an artist anywhere: and that is, upright.

Three Poems

'In Country Sleep' appeared first in a magazine which raised its hands in despair of philistine apathy so beseechingly high and so often it has since lain down from fatigue, and in a limited edition, ten copies of which are on vellum, available only to the rich who should be spending what is left of their time slimming for the eye of the needle.

'Over Sir John's Hill' has been printed in a handsome and richly appointed palace of a quarterly erected in Rome. 'In the White Giant's Thigh' is in manuscript, waiting for someone who prints strikingly few copies, at impossible prices, on fine soft Cashmere goat's hair.

These three poems will, one day, form separate parts of a long poem which is in preparation: that is to say, some of the long poem is written down on paper, some of it in a rough draft in the head, and the rest of it radiantly unworded in ambitious conjecture.

A miscellaneous writer, such as myself, who is prepared to sit in front of this cold utensil and talk, in public confidence, about his new long unwritten poem, deserves to be a successful man of letters. I used to think that once a writer became a man of letters, if only for half an hour, he was done for. And here am I now, at the very *moment* of such an odious, though respectable, danger.

Perhaps, after this, I shall become transformed into establishment; all my old doubts and worries will be over, I need bother my head about nothing except birth, death, sex, money, politics, and religion, and, jowled and wigged, aloof as a bloodhound, I may summon my former literary delinquency before me and give it a long, periodic sentence.

What can I say about the plan of a long 'poem in preparation'—I hope the quotation marks come stinging across this, to me, unbelievable lack of wires, like peeved bees—that can interest anyone save, vaguely, myself, and of course my guardian angel, a failed psycho-analyst in this life who is even now prodnosing in the air above me, casebook in claw, a little seedy and down-at-winged-heel, in the guttural consulting-rooms of space? What can I say about this long poem-to-be except that the plan of it is grand and simple and that the grandeur will seem, to many, to be purple and grandiose and the simplicity crude and sentimental? The poem is to be called 'In Country Heaven.' The godhead, the author, the milky-way farmer, the first cause, architect, lamp-lighter, quintessence, the beginning Word, the anthro-pomorphic bowler-out and blackballer, the stuff of all men, scapegoat, martyr, maker, woe-bearer—He, on top of a hill in heaven, weeps whenever, outside that state of being called his country, one of his worlds drops dead, vanishes screaming, shrivels, explodes, murders itself. And, when he weeps, Light and His tears glide down together, hand in hand. So, at the beginning of the projected poem, he weeps, and Country Heaven is suddenly dark. Bushes and owls blow out like candles. And the countrymen of heaven crouch all together under the hedges and, among themselves in the tear-salt darkness, surmise which world, which star, which of their late, turning homes, in the skies has gone for ever. And this time, spreads the heavenly hedgerow rumour, it is the Earth. The Earth has killed itself. It is black, petrified, wizened, poisoned, burst; insanity has blown it rotten; and no creatures at all, joyful, despairing, cruel, kind, dumb, afire, loving, dull, shortly and brutishly hunt their days down like enemies on that corrupted face. And, one by one, those heavenly hedgerow-men who once were of the Earth call to one another, through the long night, Light and His tears falling, what they remember, what they sense in the submerged wilderness and on the exposed hair's breadth of the mind, what they feel trembling on the nerves of a nerve, what they know in their Edenie hearts, of that self-called place. They remember places, fears, loves, exultation, misery, animal joy, ignorance, and mysteries, all *we* know and do not know.

The poem is made of these tellings. And the poem becomes, at last, an affirmation of the beautiful and terrible worth of the Earth. It grows into a praise of what is and what could be on this lump in the skies. It is a poem about happiness.

I do not expect that a first hearing of the three separate poems I am going to read can give any idea of how and where they will, eventually, take their places in that lofty, pretentious, down-to-earth-and-into-the-secrets, optimistic, ludicrous, knock-me-down moony scheme. I do not yet know myself their relevance to the whole, hypothetical structure. But I do know they belong to it.

The remembered tellings, which are the components of the poem, are not all told as though they are remembered; the poem will not be a series of poems in the past tense. The memory, in all tenses, can look towards the future, can caution and admonish. The rememberer may live himself back into active participation in the remembered scene, adventure, or spiritual condition.

'Over Sir John's Hill.' Sir John's Hill is a real hill overlooking an estuary in West Wales.

Over Sir John's hill,
The hawk on fire hangs still;
In a hoisted cloud, at drop of dusk, he pulls to his claws
And gallows, up the rays of his eyes the small birds of the
bay
And the shrill child's play
Wars
Of the sparrows and such who swansing, dusk, in
wrangling hedges.
And blithely they squawk
To fiery tyburn over the wrestle of elms until
The flash the noosed hawk
Crashes, and slowly the fishing holy stalking heron
In the river Towy below bows his tilted headstone.

Flash, and the plumes crack,
And a black cap of jack-
Daws Sir John's just hill dons, and again the gulled birds
hare
To the hawk on fire, the halter height, over Towy's fins,
In a whack of wind.
There
Where the elegiac fisherbird stabs and paddles
In the pebbly dab-filled
Shallow and sedge, and 'dilly dilly,' calls the loft hawk,
'Come and be killed,'
I open the leaves of the water at a passage
Of psalms and shadows among the pincered sandcrabs
prancing

And read, in a shell,
Death clear as a buoy's bell:
All praise of the hawk on fire in hawk-eyed dusk be sung,
When his viperish fuse hangs looped with flames under the brand
Wing, and blest shall
Young
Green chickens of the bay and bushes cluck, 'dilly dilly,
Come let us die.'
We grieve as the blithe birds, never again, leave shingle and elm,
The heron and I,
I young Aesop fabling to the near night by the dingle
Of eels, saint heron hymning in the shell-hung distant

Crystal harbour vale
Where the sea cobbles sail,
And wharves of water where the walls dance and the white cranes stilt.
It is the heron and I, under judging Sir John's elmed
Hill, tell-tale the knelled
Guilt
Of the led-astray birds whom God, for their breast of whistles,
Have mercy on,
God in his whirlwind silence save, who marks the sparrows hail,
For their souls' song.
Now the heron grieves in the weeded verge. Through windows
Of dusk and water I see the tilting whispering

Heron, mirrored, go,
As the snapt feathers snow,
Fishing in the tear of the Towy. Only a hoot owl
Hollows, a grassblade blown in cupped hands, in the
looted elms
And no green cocks or hens
Shout
Now on Sir John's hill. The heron, ankling the scaly
Lowlands of the waves,
Makes all the music; and I who hear the tune of the
slow,
Wear-willow river, grave,
Before the lunge of the night, the notes on this time-
shaken
Stone for the sake of the souls of the slain birds sailing.

The next poem, 'In Country Sleep,' is divided into two parts.

I

Never and never, my girl riding far and near
In the land of the hearthstone tales, and spelled asleep,
Fear or believe that the wolf in a sheepwhite hood
Loping and bleating roughly and blithely shall leap,
My dear, my dear,
Out of a lair in the flocked leaves in the dew dipped year
To eat your heart in the house in the rosy wood.

Sleep, good, for ever, slow and deep, spelled rare and
wise,
My girl ranging the night in the rose and shire

Of the hobnail tales: no gooseherd or swine will turn
Into a homestall king or hamlet of fire
And prince of ice
To court the honeyed heart from your side before sunrise
In a spinney of ringed boys and ganders, spike and burn,

Nor the innocent lie in the rooting dingle wooed
And staved, and riven among plumes my rider weep.
From the broomed witch's spume you are shielded by fern
And flower of country sleep and the greenwood keep.
Lie fast and soothed,
Safe be and smooth from the bellows of the rushy brood.
Never, my girl, until tolled to sleep by the stern

Bell believe or fear that the rustic shade or spell
Shall harrow and snow the blood while you ride wide and near,
For who unmanningly haunts the mountain ravened eaves
Or skulks in the dell moon but moonshine echoing clear
From the starred well?
A hill touches an angel. Out of a saint's cell
The nightbird lauds through nunneries and domes of leaves

Her robin breasted tree, three Marys in the rays.
Sanctum sanctorum the animal eye of the wood
In the rain telling its beads, and the gravest ghost
The owl at its knelling. Fox and holt kneel before blood.
Now the tales praise
The star rise at pasture and nightlong the fables graze
On the lord's-table of the bowing grass. Fear most

For ever of all not the wolf in his baaing hood
Nor the tusked prince, in the ruttish farm, at the rind
And mire of love, but the Thief as meek as the dew.
The country is holy: O bide in that country kind,
Know the green good,
Under the prayer wheeling moon in the rosy wood
Be shielded by chant and flower and gay may you

Lie in grace. Sleep spelled at rest in the lowly house
In the squirrel nimble grove, under linen and thatch
And star: held and blessed, though you scour the high four
Winds, from the dousing shade and the roarer at the latch,
Cool in your vows.
Yet out of the beaked, web dark and the pouncing boughs
Be you sure the Thief will seek a way sly and sure

And sly as snow and meek as dew blown to the thorn,
This night and each vast night until the stern bell talks
In the tower and tolls to sleep over the stalls
Of the hearthstone tales my own, lost love; and the soul walks
The waters shorn.
This night and each night since the falling star you were born,
Ever and ever he finds a way, as the snow falls,

As the rain falls, hail on the fleece, as the vale mist rides
Through the haygold stalls, as the dew falls on the wind-
Milled dust of the apple tree and the pounded islands
Of the morning leaves, as the star falls, as the winged

Apple seed glides,
And falls, and flowers in the yawning wound at our sides,
As the world falls, silent as the cyclone of silence.

II

Night and the reindeer on the clouds above the haycocks
And the wings of the great roc ribboned for the fair!
The leaping saga of prayer! And high, there, on the hare-
Heeled winds the rooks
Cawing from their black bethels soaring, the holy books
Of birds! Among the cocks like fire the red fox

Burning! Night and the vein of birds in the winged, sloe wrist
Of the wood! Pastoral beat of blood through the laced leaves!
The stream from the priest black wristed spinney and sleeves
Of thistling frost
Of the nightingale's din and tale! The upgiven ghost
Of the dingle torn to singing and the surpliced

Hill of cypresses! The din and tale in the skimmed
Yard of the buttermilk rain on the pail! The sermon
Of blood! The bird loud vein! The saga from mermen
To seraphim
Leaping! The gospel rooks! All tell, this night, of him
Who comes as red as the fox and sly as the heeled wind.

Illumination of music! the lulled black-backed
Gull, on the wave with sand in its eyes! And the foal moves

Through the shaken greensward lake, silent, on moon-
    shod hooves,
                                        In the winds' wakes.
Music of elements, that a miracle makes!
Earth, air, water, fire, singing into the white act,

The haygold haired, my love asleep, and the rift blue
Eyed, in the haloed house, in her rareness and hilly
High riding, held and blessed and true, and so stilly
                                        Lying the sky
Might cross its planets, the bell weep, night gather her
    eyes,
The Thief fall on the dead like the willy nilly dew,

Only for the turning of the earth in her holy
Heart! Slyly, slowly, hearing the wound in her side go
Round the sun, he comes to my love like the resigned
    snow, .
                                        And truly he
Flows to the strand of flowers like the dew's ruly sea,
And surely he sails like the ship shape clouds. Oh he

Comes resigned to my love to steal not her tide raking
Wound, nor her riding high, nor her eyes, nor kindled
    hair,
But her faith that each vast night and the saga of prayer
                                        He comes to take
Her faith that this last night for his unsacred sake
He comes to leave her in the lawless sun awaking

Naked and forsaken to grieve he will not come.
Ever and ever by all your vows believe and fear

My dear this night he comes and night without end my dear
Since you were born:
And you shall wake, from country sleep, this dawn and each first dawn,
Your faith as deathless as the outcry of the ruled sun.

'In the White Giant's Thigh,' just written, will, no doubt, have many small details altered before it is printed, but the general feel and sound of it will remain the same even when I have cleared up some of its more obviously overlush, arch and exuberant, mauve *gauche* moments.

Through throats where many rivers meet, the curlews cry,
Under the conceiving moon, on the high chalk hill,
And there this night I walk in the white giant's thigh
Where barren as boulders women lie longing still

To labour and love though they lay down long ago.
Through throats where many rivers meet, the women pray,
Pleading in the waded bay for the seed to flow
Though the names on their weed grown stones are rained away,

And alone in the night's eternal, curving act
They yearn with tongues of curlews for the unconceived
And immemorial sons of the cudgelling, hacked

Hill. Who once in gooseskin winter loved all ice leaved
In the courters' lanes, or twined in the ox roasting sun
In the wains tonned so high that the wisps of the hay
Clung to the pitching clouds, or gay with any one
Young as they in the after milking moonlight lay

Under the lighted shapes of faith and their moonshade
Petticoats galed high, or shy with the rough riding boys,
Now clasp me to their grains in the gigantic glade,

Who once, green countries since, were a hedgerow of
joys.
Time by, their dust was flesh the swineherd rooted sly,
Flared in the reek of the wiving sty with the rush
Light of his thighs, spreadeagle to the dunghill sky,
Or with their orchard man in the core of the sun's bush
Rough as cows' tongues and thrashed with brambles their
buttermilk
Manes, under his quenchless summer barbed gold to the
bone,

Or rippling soft in the spinney moon as the silk
And ducked and draked white lake that harps to a hail
stone.
Who once were a bloom of wayside brides in the hawed
house
And heard the lewd, wooed field flow to the coming frost,
The scurrying, furred small friars squeal, in the dowse
Of day, in the thistle aisles, till the white owl crossed

Their breast, the vaulting does roister, the horned bucks
climb
Quick in the wood at love, where a torch of foxes foams,
All birds and beasts of the linked night uproar and chime

And the mole snout blunt under his pilgrimage of domes,
Or, butter fat goosegirls, bounced in a gambo bed,
Their breasts full of honey, under their gander king
Trounced by his wings in the hissing shippen, long dead
And gone that barley dark where their clogs danced in
the spring,
And their firefly hairpins flew, and the ricks ran round—
(But nothing bore, no mouthing babe to the veined hives
Hugged, and barren and bare on Mother Goose's ground
They with the simple Jacks were a boulder of wives)—

Now curlew cry me down to kiss the mouths of their
dust.

The dust of their kettles and clocks swings to and fro
Where the hay rides now or the bracken kitchens rust
As the arc of the billhooks that flashed the hedges low
And cut the birds' boughs that the minstrel sap ran red.
They from houses where the harvest kneels, hold me
hard,
Who heard the tall bell sail down the Sundays of the dead
And the rain wring out its tongues on the faded yard,
Teach me the love that is evergreen after the fall leaved
Grave, after Belovéd on the grass gulfed cross is scrubbed
Off by the sun and Daughters no longer grieved
Save by their long desires in the fox cubbed
Streets or hungering in the crumbled wood: to these
Hale dead and deathless do the women of the hill
Love for ever meridian through the courters' trees

And the daughters of darkness flame like Fawkes fires
still.

On Poetry

I agree that music-hall songs can be good poetry—so can limericks, drawing- or tap-room—but I don't think cracker mottoes, etc., ever have been. I think, Stephens, you must be pulling my (comparatively) young leg. The younger generation used to be called, by their elders, flippant. Not any longer. It's we, now, who deprecate their flippancy. I feel rather like the little pedantically reproving girl addressing Matthew Arnold in Max Beerbohm's picture: 'Why, Uncle Matthew, oh why, will not you be always wholly serious?' I'm all for taking the *serious* nonsense out of one's appreciation of poetry; I hate, as much as you do, the hushed voice and hats-off attitude, but I don't like the double-bluffing approach that pretends to think that 'I'm one of the ruins that Cromwell knocked about a bit' is better poetry than, say, the serious, unfashionable work of Cowper or Francis Thompson. It's just very different poetry. . . .

Almost anything one says about poetry is as true and important as *anything* else that *anyone* else has said. Some people react *physically* to the magic of poetry, to the moments, that is, of authentic revelation, of the communication, the *sharing*, at its highest level, of personal experience; they say they feel a twanging at their tear-ducts, or a prickling of the scalp, or a tickling of the spine, or tremors in what they hope is their heart. Others say that they have a kind of a sort of a vague feeling somewhere that 'this is the real stuff.' Others claim that their 'purely aesthetic emotion' was induced by certain assonances and alliterations. And some are content merely to say, as they said of the first cinematographic picture, 'By God, it moves.' And so, of course, by God, it does, for that is another name for the magic beyond definition. . . .

The magic in a poem is always accidental. No poet would labour intensively upon the intricate craft of poetry unless he hoped that, suddenly, the accident of magic would occur. He *has* to agree with Chesterton that the miraculous thing about miracles is that they *do* sometimes happen. And the best poem is that whose worked-upon unmagical passages come closest, in texture and intensity, to those moments of magical accident. . . .

. . . And there's this to be said too. Poetry, to a poet, is the most rewarding work in the world. A good poem is a contribution to reality. The world is never the same once a good poem has been added to it. A good poem helps to change the shape and significance of the universe, helps to extend everyone's knowledge of himself and the world around him. . . .

I think there's an inverted snobbery—and a suggestion of bad logic—in being proud of the fact that one's poems sell very badly. *Of course*, nearly *every* poet wants his poems to be read by as many people as possible. Craftsmen don't put their products in the attic. And contempt for the public, which is composed of potential readers, is contempt for the profound usefulness of your own craft. Go on thinking that you don't *need* to be read, and you'll find that it may become quite true: no one *will* feel the need to read it, because it is written for yourself alone; and the public won't feel any impulse to gate-crash such a private party. Moreover, to take no notice of the work of your contemporaries is to disregard a whole *vital* part of the world you live in, and necessarily to devitalize your own work: to narrow its scope and possibilities: to be half dead as you write. . . .

What's more, a poet is a poet for such a very tiny bit of his life; for the rest, he is a human being, one of whose responsibilities is to know and feel, as much as he can, all that is moving around and within him, so that his poetry, when he comes to write it, can be his attempt at an expression of the summit of man's experience on this very peculiar and, in 1946, this apparently hell-bent earth.

NOTES

No doubt many of these notes will be superfluous to the Welsh reader, but they have been included in the hope that they may be of some help to those who have no knowledge of the Welsh background of many of the pieces in this volume.

Reminiscences of Childhood

First broadcast: 15th February 1943. B.B.C. Welsh Home Service.

Repeated: 6th May 1953. B.B.C. Welsh Home Service.

Printed in *The Listener* (edited) 25th February 1943, vol. 29, pp. 246–7.

When this talk was first written Thomas was working as a script writer for a film company in London. In view of the statements which have appeared in various places since his death, it is necessary to emphasize that he was at no time a member of the staff of the British Broadcasting Corporation.

In this talk he is describing his home town—Swansea—where he was born on 27th October 1914, at 5 Cwmdonkin Drive on the hillside overlooking Cwmdonkin Park and the sea—the 'splendid curving shore' of Swansea Bay.

The 'Hunchback in the Park' poem included in this talk had previously been published in *Life and Letters Today*, October 1941. The full stop at the end of the first verse (p. 11) is printed according to Thomas's own version for broadcasting. So also is the order of the third and fourth lines in the fourth verse.

I have printed both versions of this talk, for they give, I believe, an interesting insight into his painstaking revisions, and the changed outlook of more mature years.

Quite Early One Morning

First broadcast: 31st August 1945. B.B.C. Welsh Home Service.

Repeated: 17th June 1953. B.B.C. Welsh Home Service.

The topographical features of this talk are derived from New Quay, a small seaside town on the Cardiganshire coast, where Thomas spent some time during the war years. It is perched precariously on the cliff side, with its main street running down precipitously to the old stone quay 'shouldering out' to the sea.

(Page 15) *sober as Sunday*—a reference to the Sunday closing of public-houses in Wales.

(Page 16) *Ben Davies*—a famous Welsh tenor born in the last century who was still a household name in Wales when the author was a young man.

(Page 18) *bilingual sea*—Wales is still a bilingual country; although Thomas himself knew no Welsh, yet he, like every other writer in Wales, was always conscious of this bilingual background.

(Page 18) *laver-bread*—a delicacy made of seaweed peculiar to the Swansea district.

(Page 20) *B.A., Aber.*—graduate of the Aberystwyth College of the University of Wales.

In the repeated broadcast of this talk Thomas changed some of the names; why, I cannot say.

Clara Tivy Jenkins became Clara Tawe Jenkins.

Parchedig (Reverend) Frogmar Evans became Parchedig Thomas Evans.

Captain Tiny Evans's ship *Casper* became the *Kidwelly*.

He also deleted one verse at the last moment, in the studio, with the comment: 'Oh God!' It read:

I can see the Atlantic from my bed where I always lie,
Night and day, night and day, eating my bread and slops;
The quiet cripple staring at the sea and the sky;
I shall lie here till the sky goes out and the sea stops.

MEMORIES OF CHRISTMAS

First broadcast: 16th December 1945. B.B.C. Welsh Home Service (Children's Hour).

Printed in *The Listener*: 20th December 1945, vol. 34, 734–5.

Another slightly longer version of this talk was printed in the December 1950 issue of *Harper's Bazaar*.

HOLIDAY MEMORY

First broadcast: 25th October 1946. B.B.C. Welsh Home Service.

Repeated: 2nd January 1947. B.B.C. Third Programme.

Printed in *The Listener*: 7th November 1946, vol. 36, 634–5.

(Page 31) *trams that hissed like ganders*—in Thomas's boyhood days Swansea possessed a network of noisy electric trams; they have now disappeared.

(Page 37) *mumbling bay*—a pun on Mumbles Head which marks the westward limit of Swansea Bay.

HOW TO BEGIN A STORY

First broadcast: 8th October 1946. B.B.C. Home Service.

Printed in *The Listener*: 17th October 1946, vol. 36, p. 508.

THE CRUMBS OF ONE MAN'S YEAR

First broadcast: 27th December 1946. B.B.C. Home Service.

Printed in *The Listener*: 2nd January 1947, vol. 37, pp. 28–9.

THE FESTIVAL EXHIBITION, 1951

First broadcast: 5th June 1951. B.B.C. Welsh Home Service.

The visit to the Festival Exhibition was made at the request of the B.B.C. I had no difficulty in persuading him to make the long journey from Laugharne to London. 'I'd just love it,' he said with boyish enthusiasm.

THE INTERNATIONAL EISTEDDFOD

First broadcast: 13th July 1953. B.B.C. Welsh Home Service.

This Eisteddfod, or competitive festival, held every year at Llangollen, in North Wales, is the counterpart of the Welsh National Eisteddfod. The national festival is a closed shop for writers, poets, and playwrights who use the Welsh language as their medium. The International Festival confines itself to music and draws competitors from all over the world.

In July 1953 I took Thomas, with his wife Caitlin and little daughter Aeronwy, to spend a week at Llangollen, and to report his impressions in a radio talk.

This trip with Thomas to the International Eisteddfod gave me an opportunity of studying his method of collecting material for these radio talks. The week was spent in apparently aimless meanderings through the crowded streets of the town, occasional half-hours in the Eisteddfod marquee, and many hours standing at the bars of the far from few pubs of the town. Now and then, while standing at the bar, Thomas would tear open an empty cigarette carton, take out a stub of pencil from his pocket, and behind the shelter of a friendly pint he would scribble a few words, sometimes just a single word, and deposit it in the depths of his capacious coat pocket. By the end of the week he had a harvest of these scribbled phrases. There was a moment of panic in the car on the way home when he thought that he had lost these notes. His jottings were afterwards copied out on to a sheet of paper, and then the task of writing began. He spent the whole of Sunday and most of Monday at this work, and arrived at the studio about an hour before the broadcast with his talk carefully written out in his boyish hand. I remember that it was about three minutes short, but there was no question of adding to it; and there was to be no hurried scribbling in the studio.

(Page 59) *Dinas Brân*—an ancient fortress which stands, in ruins, high up on the hill overlooking the town and vale of Llangollen.

A Visit to America

First broadcast: 30th March 1954. B.B.C. Welsh Home Service.
Printed in *The Listener*: 22nd April 1954, vol. 51, pp. 692–3.

This talk was recorded at the Swansea studios of the B.B.C. during the week in which he left Swansea and Laugharne for London, on the first part of his ill-fated journey to America. The talk had been scheduled for broadcasting on a date which turned out to be the day of his funeral at Laugharne.

LAUGHARNE

First broadcast (in part): 5th November 1953. B.B.C. Welsh Home Service.

This short piece, recorded at the same time as 'A Visit to America,' was included in a documentary programme on Laugharne broadcast from the school hall of the town. There was an audience at the broadcast, and Mrs Dylan Thomas was present. At the end of the programme, in a short speech of thanks to the townspeople, I paid tribute to the great poet who lived among them. After I sat down Mrs Thomas turned to me to say that she had just received news by cable that her husband was lying unconscious in an American hospital.

RETURN JOURNEY

First broadcast: 15th June 1947. B.B.C. Home Service. Produced at Cardiff by P. H. Burton.

Repeated: 20th June 1947. B.B.C. Welsh Home Service.
28th June 1947. B.B.C. Third Programme.
13th August 1947. B.B.C. General Overseas Service.
22nd August 1947. B.B.C. Home Service.
14th February 1951. B.B.C. Home Service.
21st February 1954. B.B.C. Welsh Home Service.

(Page 74) *Tawe water*—River Tawe flows into the Bristol Channel at Swansea, giving the town its Welsh name, *Abertawe*.

(Page 74) *Swansea china*—Swansea was once famous for its pottery, and pieces of Swansea china are held in high esteem by the collector.

(Page 74) *a egg*—an idiosyncrasy of the native Swansea dialect. Cf. *a* owl, p. 90.

(Page 76) *an open-air performance of 'Electra'*—*Electra* was played by the Swansea Little Theatre in a garden at Sketty Green in 1933. Thomas was an active member of this dramatic society and after the performance of the play wrote a poem:

A woman wails her dead among the trees,
Under the green roof grieves the living;
The living sun laments the dying skies,
Lamenting falls. Pity Electra's loving.

Of all Orestes' continent of pride
Dust in the little country of an urn,
Of Agamemnon and his kingly blood
That cries along her veins. No sun or moon
Shall lamp the raven darkness of her face,
And no Aegean wind cool her cracked heart;
There are no sea-caves deeper than her eyes
Day treads the trees, and she the cavernous night.

Among the trees the language of the dead
Sounds rich with life, out of a painted mask;
The queen is slain; Orestes' hands drip blood;
And women talk of horror to the dusk.

There can be few tears left: Electra wept
A country's tears, and voiced a world's despair
At flesh that perishes and blood that's spilt,
And love that goes down like a flower.

Pity the living who are last, alone;
The dead in Hades have their host of friends;
The dead queen walketh with Mycenae's king
Through Hades' groves and the Eternal Lands.

Pity Electra loveless, she whose grief
Drowns and is drowned, who utters to the stars
Her syllables, and to the gods her love;
Pity the poor unpitied who are strange with tears.

Among the garden trees a pigeon calls,
And knows no woe that these sad players mouth
Of evil oracles and funeral ills;
A pigeon calls, and women talk of death.

The music for this play was written by Daniel Jones.

(Page 76) *Uplands*—the part of the town where Thomas was born and brought up.

(Page 79) *Vetch*—'Swansea Town's' soccer ground.

(Page 80) *Gymanfa Ganu*—Hymn-singing Festival.

(Page 81) *Post*—The *South Wales Evening Post*, the Swansea evening paper on which Thomas worked as a junior reporter.

(Page 82) *Dan Jones, Vernon Watkins, etc.*

Many of the names in this talks-feature are the names of real people. Dan Jones is the Swansea composer, and a close friend of the poet. He also figures prominently in Thomas's volume of short stories, *Portrait of the Artist as a Young Dog*. Vernon Watkins, another Swansea poet of distinction, was also a close friend.

In February 1941 Swansea suffered a three nights' blitz. The shopping centre of the town was demolished, and the old landmarks of shops, pubs, and cafés, which Thomas knew so well, were obliterated. However, with Joyceian regard for detail, Thomas consulted the borough architect's maps of the town in order to check his memory.

Wilfred Owen

Broadcast: 27th July 1946. B.B.C. Eastern Service.

Thomas only quotes *part* of the preface to Owen's volume of poems.

Walter de la Mare as a Prose Writer

First broadcast: 30th November 1946. B.B.C. Third Programme.

Repeated: 8th December 1946. B.B.C. Third Programme.

Sir Philip Sidney

Broadcast: 24th January 1947. B.B.C. West of England Home Service.

This was the first in the third series of talks under the title 'Literature in the West (of England).'

A Dearth of Comic Writers

Broadcast: 14th February 1948. B.B.C. Light Programme.

This material has been extracted from a conversation between the poet and Arthur Calder Marshall.

The words in square brackets have been inserted by the editor.

The English Festival of Spoken Poetry

Broadcast: 30th July 1948. B.B.C. Third Programme.
Printed in *The Listener*: 5th August 1948, p. 205.

On Reading One's Own Poems

Broadcast: 24th September 1949. B.B.C. Third Programme.

The introduction to a reading of his own poems.

Welsh Poets

Broadcast: 5th January 1946. B.B.C. Eastern Service. Produced by John Arlott.

The comments on Wilfred Owen in this talk have been omitted in favour of the more detailed discussion of Owen's poetry to be found elsewhere in this volume. I have also left out some humorous comment on two minor Welsh poets, John Dyer, 'still remembered, if only as a name, by those who read poetry for a degree and by those who live near Grongar Hill,' and Sir Lewis Morris, 'who wrote nearly a thousand poems, many of them long, lyrics, idylls, tragedies, odes of welcome to the Trades Union Congress, Swansea, 1901, triolets in ladies' albums, elegies on the deaths of statesmen . . . we must read him together some time!'

Wales and the Artist

Broadcast: 24th October 1949. B.B.C. Welsh Home Service. Produced by John Griffiths.

Wales and the Artist

An extract from his introductory remarks to a talks-feature on 'Swansea and the Arts.' With him in the studio were Vernon Watkins, Daniel Jones, Alfred Janes, and John Prichard. It may be of interest to record his tribute to Vernon Watkins, the distinguished Swansea poet:

I think him to be the most profound and greatly accomplished Welshman writing poems in English, and he is one of the few poets I know, intensely occupied with his craft, who happily makes a living in a way that has nothing to do with words. So many writers, because their own serious writing does not pay, live by writing about writing, lecturing about writing, reviewing other writers, script writing, advertising, journalizing, boiling pots for the chain-store publishers: Vernon Watkins writes nothing but poems. Very properly, he makes his living by other people's money: in a bank. He is proof against the dangers (so tempting to poets, such as myself, who are not qualified to extract their livelihoods other than by the use of language), the dangers of mellifluous periphrasis, otiose solipsism, the too-easy spin and flow of the paid word.

Three Poems

Broadcast: 25th September 1950. B.B.C. Third Programme. Produced by Douglas Cleverdon.

'In Country Sleep' was first printed (in this country) in *Horizon*, December 1947.

'Over Sir John's Hill' was printed in *Botteghe Oscure*, November 1950.

These poems are printed in *Collected Poems* as three independent poems, and vary only slightly from the versions read in this programme.

On Poetry

Broadcast: 18th June 1946. B.B.C. Light Programme.

These extracts have been taken from the script of a discussion with James Stephens, in a broadcast, 'Poets on Poetry,' in the series 'Books and Writers.' Gerald Bullett acted as chairman.